Praise for *Vanessa & Virginia*

Barnes & Noble Discover selection • Indie Next List pick

"Superb . . . *Vanessa and Virginia* is one of the few recent reads I haven't wanted to end." —**Sonoma Country Life**

"*Vanessa and Virginia* captures the sisters' seesaw dynamic as they vacillate between protecting and hurting each other." —*Christian Science Monitor*

"A delectable little book for anyone who ever admired the Bloomsbury group . . . a genuine treat for Bloomsbury fans." —*Publishers Weekly*

"A beautifully written exploration of tortured talent, sibling conflicts, domestic discord, disappointed love affairs, and emotional despair." —*Booklist*

"A beautifully written novel . . . Sellers achieves a believable psychological reality in the figure of Vanessa . . . [whose] memory moves across years and through moments with sensitivity and grace, so that the reader is seamlessly transported from place to place, event to event, feeling to feeling . . . Woolf scholar [Sellers] is meticulous in her attention to facts and details . . . [She] creates a believable reality which the reader (Bloomsbury expert or not) can fully appreciate. Sellers' command of her material, her ability to create Post-impressionist pictures with words, and her mastery of the difficult pastiche form, means that her work stands as a literary success in its own right." —*Virginia Woolf Bulletin*

"I was impressed by the beauty of the language, by the compression, by the way that the technique . . . creates such a resonant text for readers—even for readers who have themselves read a great deal of Woolf."

—Melba Cuddy-Keane, author of *Virginia Woolf, the Intellectual and the Public Sphere*

"Deftly, apparently effortlessly, Susan Sellers's novel of love, art, and sexual jealousy gives us convincing and intimate access to the relationship between two remarkable sisters. At once pellucid and sophisticated, *Vanessa and Virginia* is quite simply a pleasure to read." —Robert Crawford, author of *Full Volume*

"Beautiful, haunting . . . I can think of no other work that is as searching, or as revealing in its exploration of the family life or of the complex dynamic of sibling and artistic rivalry of these two artists." —John Burnside, author of *A Lie About My Father*

"This biographical novel shimmers with brilliant prose yet grounds readers with skillful and accurate period detail. *Vanessa and Virginia* is a lyrical risk-taking novel, and the risks pay off." —Sally Cline, author of *Zelda Fitzgerald: Her Voice in Paradise*

"Ravishing, literate, and fascinating."

—Caroline Leavitt, author of *Girls in Trouble*

Vanessa &
Virginia

Susan Sellers

Mariner Books
Houghton Mifflin Harcourt
BOSTON   NEW YORK

First Mariner Books edition 2010

Copyright © 2009 by Susan Sellers

First published in Great Britain in 2008 by Ravens Press

www.hmhbooks.com

Library of Congress Cataloging-in-Publication Data
Sellers, Susan.
Vanessa and Virginia / Susan Sellers. — 1st ed.
p. cm.
ISBN 978-0-15-101474-3
1. Bell, Vanessa, 1879–1961 — Fiction. 2. Woolf, Virginia, 1882–1941 —
Fiction. 3. Sisters — Fiction. 4. Women artists — Fiction. 5. Women
authors — Fiction. 6. Bloomsbury group — Fiction. 7. London
(England) — Intellectual life — 20th century — Fiction. I. Title.
PR6119.E45V36 2009
823'.92 — dc22   2008026085

ISBN 978-0-547-26338-0 (pbk.)

Book design by Melissa Lotfy
Text is set in Electra.

Printed in the United States of America

DOC 10 9 8 7 6 5 4 3 2 1

For Jeremy and Ben Thurlow,
with love

1

I AM LYING ON MY BACK ON THE GRASS. THOBY IS LYING next to me, his warm flank pressing into my side. My eyes are open and I am watching the clouds, tracing giants, castles, fabulous winged beasts as they chase each other across the sky. Something light tickles my cheek. I raise myself onto my elbow and catch hold of the grass stalk in Thoby's hand. He jerks away from me, and soon we are pummeling and giggling until I scarcely know which of the tumbling legs and arms are Thoby's and which are mine. When we stop at last, Thoby's face is on my chest. I feel the weight of his head against my ribs. His hair is golden in the sunlight and as I look up I see the blazing whiteness of an angel. I loop my arm round Thoby's neck. For the first time in my life I know what bliss means.

A shadow falls. My angel disappears. I recognize your snake-green eyes. You want to lie between us and when I push you away you jump up and whisper in Thoby's ear. He lifts his head and looks at you. I see from his expression that your words have captured him. I know that you will lure him away with one of your daredevil plans. I roll over and press my face into the grass. The blades prickle my eyelids and I concentrate on the sharpness. When I turn round again the two of you have gone. I sit up and spot Thoby perching precariously on top of the garden wall. His hand clutches at the branches overhead as he tries to steady himself. I hear him shrieking with daring and fear. I want to shout to him to come and play in the grass with me. Then I watch you catch hold of Thoby's leg and pull yourself up beside him. You wobble for a moment before you find your balance. I know that now you will turn and wave to me in triumph. I lie back on the grass, feigning indifference. Not for the world will I let you see my tears.

I lift my head from the page and look out the window. Sunlight shivers on the glass. For a moment I see your face as it was then, impish, grinning at me as I write. The light dissolves and you disappear. I am left staring at the empty pane. My memories are as tangled as the reels of thread and fragments of cloth in Mother's sewing basket, which I loved to tip out and sort on the nursery floor: colored ribbons, stray buttons, a triangle of purple lace.

Mother. She enters the nursery like a queen. We, her troops, present ourselves for her inspection, fidgeting as we wait in line for our turn. Her hair is parted in the middle and tied at the back of her neck in a net. She wears a black dress, which rustles like leaves as she moves about the room, gathering up the damp clothes that have been draped over the fireguard, sweeping the scattered pieces of a puzzle back into their box. Her ringed fingers dance as she talks to the nursemaids. I learn the questions she asks them by heart. Later I will set out my dolls and quiz them in her clear round voice about castor oil and the mending. I practice standing with my head erect and my back straight until my shoulders feel as if they are pinned in a press. Finally, Mother seats herself in the chair by the fire and calls us to her.

Always, Thoby goes first. I watch him pulled into the curve of Mother's arm, closing my eyes to imagine the silky feel of her dress, her smell of lavender and eau de nil. When I open my eyes her fingers are stroking his hair. I do not question why it is always Thoby who is first, or why, when Adrian is born, he takes his place after Thoby. I sense that this is the order of things and that here my wishes count for little. Yet when Thoby is relinquished with a kiss and Mother holds out her hand to you it is as if a promise has been broken. My stomach clenches and a hot spurt of indignation surges to my cheeks. I am the eldest. I should come before you. As Mother lifts you onto her knee your dimpled hands reach for the ribbon she wears at her throat. Checked by her reproving frown, you lean forward and kiss her. Her smile is like sunshine on a winter's afternoon. You seem to spend an eternity in her arms. Your palms clap together in a rhyme of pat-a-cake, and when Mother praises you I wonder what would happen if a spark from the fire were to catch your petticoat. I picture your clothes igniting and your red hair blazing and Mother in her alarm hugging me to her breast.

There is a knock on the door. Ellen, slightly breathless from the stairs, holds out a card on a tray. Mother sighs and reaches for the card. When she has finished reading it she puts it back on the tray and tells Ellen that she will come straight down. She lifts you from her lap and with a final instruction to the nursemaids follows Ellen onto the landing.

I stare after her. You crawl toward me and your hand reaches for the buckle on my shoe. Quick as lightning, I kick back with my heel and trap your fingers under the sole. Your howl voices what I feel. I count to five before I lift my foot. Then I reach down and pick you up and carry you to the chair Mother sat in. I settle you on my lap and rock you backward and forward until the soft lullaby of your breathing tells me you are asleep.

It is my half sister Stella who first puts a piece of chalk in my hand. She and I share a birthday. I rummage in her pocket and pull out the package I know is there. It is wrapped in brown paper that crinkles as I turn it over in my hands. Inside are six stubby colored fingers. Stella takes a board she has concealed under her arm and draws on it. I am amazed by the wavy line that appears and reach up to try the chalk for myself. I spend the morning absorbed in my new pursuit. Though my hands are clumsy, I persevere until the board is covered. I am fascinated by the way my marks cross and join with each other, opening tiny triangles, diamonds, rectangles between the lines. When I have finished I sit back and stare at my achievement. I have transformed the dull black of the board into a rainbow of colors, a hail of shapes that jump about as I look. I am so pleased with what I have done that I hide the board away. I do not want to share my discovery with anyone.

We are in the hall dressed and ready for our walk. At our request Ellen lifts us onto the chair by the mirror so that we can see the reflections we make. Our faces are inexact replicas of each other, as if the painter were trying to capture the same person from different angles. Your face is prettier than mine, your features finer, your eyes a whirligig of quick lights. You are my natural ally in my dealings with the world. I adore the way you watch me accomplish the things you cannot yet achieve. I do not yet see the frustration, the desire to catch up and topple me that darkens your awe.

"Who do you like best, Mother or Father?" Your question comes like a bolt out of the blue. I hold the jug of warm water suspended in midair and look at you. You are kneeling on the bathmat, shiny-skinned and rosy from the steam. The ends of your hair are wet and you have a towel draped round your shoulders. I am dazzled by the audacity of your question. Slowly I let the water from the jug pour into the bath.

"Mother." I lean back into the warmth.

You consider my answer, squeezing the damp from your hair.

"I prefer Father."

"Father?" I sit up quickly. "How can you possibly like Father best? He's always so difficult to please."

"At least he's not vague." You spin round and look at me directly. I sense that you are enjoying this discussion.

"But Mother is . . ." I search for my word. I think of the arch of her neck as she walks into a room, the way the atmosphere changes as she seats herself at table.

"Is what?" Your eyes are daring me now.

"Beautiful." I say the word quietly.

"What does that count for?" You do nothing to hide your contempt. "Mother doesn't know as much as Father, she doesn't read as much. At least when Father settles on something you know he isn't going to be called away."

I want to rally, hit back, protest how self-centered Father is. I want to declare Mother's goodness, proclaim her unstinting

5

sense of duty, her ability to restore order when all is in disarray. Instead I stare in silence at the water. From the corner of my eye I can see that you are smiling.

"Well at least we needn't fight about who we like." Sure of your victory, your tone now is conciliatory. I get out of the bath and wrap myself in a towel. As so often happens, our argument has made me miserable. I press my forehead against the glass of the window and watch the branches of the trees make criss-cross patterns against the sky. I do not like this sifting through our feelings, weighing Mother's merits and Father's faults as if the answer to our lives were a simple question of arithmetic. Not for the first time, I find myself fearing where your cleverness will lead.

I want to convey the aura of those days. Father's controlling presence, the sound of his pacing in the study above us, his clamorous, insistent groans. Mother sitting writing at her desk, preoccupied, elusive. I visualize the scene as if it were a painting. The colors are dark — black, gray, russet, wine red — with flashes of crimson from the fire. At the top of the picture are flecks of silver sky. The children kneel in the foreground. Mother, Father, our half brothers George and Gerald stand in a ring behind us, their figures monumental and restraining. Though our faces are indistinct it is possible to make out our outlines. Thoby's arm reaches across mine, in search of a toy, perhaps, a cotton reel or wooden train. Laura hides behind Thoby, Stella's arm curled round her in a sheltering arc. Adrian, still a baby, lies asleep in his crib. You are in the center of the picture. You seem to be painted in a different palette. Your hair is threaded with the red of the fire, your dress streaked with silver from the sky. You leap out from the monotone gloom of the rest. I cannot tell if this prominence has been forced on you, or if it is something you have sought for yourself.

"Do pay attention, Vanessa!" Mother's rebuke startles me from my reverie and I struggle to focus on what she is telling us. She is teaching us history. Her back is as straight as a rod and her hands are folded demurely in her lap. This, too, is part of our lesson. She wishes us to learn that we must be controlled and attentive at all times. My mind skates over the list of names she is reading aloud to us. There is a picture of a crown at the top of her page and without meaning to I lose myself in its delicate crenelations.

"Vanessa! This is the second time of telling! You will please stand up and recite the kings and queens of England in order and without error!" I jump out of my chair. Your eyes are fixed on me and I sense you willing me to remember. I stammer the names of William and Henry and Stephen then grind to a stop. Before Mother can scold, you come to my rescue.

"Please, I have a question." We both look at Mother, who nods.

"Is it true Elizabeth the First was the greatest queen England has ever known? Was she truly — a superlative monarch?" Mother smiles at your eloquence and I slink back into my chair, dejected as well as relieved. You have your permission to proceed and your eyes shine in triumph. I know that nothing will stop you now.

"Do you suppose it was because she was a woman that she achieved so much? I mean, it's true, isn't it, that she never married? I suppose there wasn't a king who was good enough for her. If she had married she would have been busy having children and so wouldn't have had time for her affairs of state. The people called her 'Gloriana' and she had her own motto."

"'*Semper eadem*'!" Father stands in the doorway, applauding your performance. He has the book from which he is teaching us mathematics under his arm. "'Always the same.' It was the motto she had inscribed on her tomb. So it's Elizabeth the First, is it? The Virgin Queen. In that case, perhaps you had better come with me and we will see what we can find for you in my library." You slip from your chair and take the hand Father holds out to you. I see the skip in your walk as you accompany him out of the room. The door closes behind you and I turn my attention back to Mother. I try not to hear her sigh as she begins to reread the list of names.

I thumb the pages of the family photograph album and stop at a portrait of Laura, Father's daughter by his first marriage. She is nine, ten, perhaps, and her ringleted hair cascades over her shoulders. Her face is turned away from the camera and she clasps a small doll in her arms. It is impossible to tell her expression.

You never ridiculed Laura, I remember. Once when Thoby tried to imitate her stammering and pretended to throw his food in the fire you were so angry you slapped him. He turned to you in disbelief but the indignation on your face was real.

The day Laura was sent away you stayed in our room. It was one of your "curse" days, and when I went to see if you wanted anything I found you lying with your face buried in your pillow. As I tiptoed toward your bed you turned to look at me.

"Have they sent her to a madhouse?" I did not know the answer any more than you but shook my head.

"How could they?" I saw then the anguish in your eyes. As

I put my arm around you it was my fear as well as yours I was shielding.

We lie in our beds watching the darkness. Though we plead for a crack to be left in the curtains they are pulled tight against the certainty of drafts. I close my eyes to conjure the moonlight and listen for Mother's footsteps on the stairs. There are guests tonight and we have helped her dress. I fastened her pearl necklace carefully round her neck and she promised to come and kiss us goodnight. I imagine her sitting at the table, handing round the plates of soup. If the dinner is a success she will tell us about her labors. She will describe the fidgety young man who must be coaxed into the conversation, and the woman whose talk of ailments has to be curtailed to avert alarm. She will tell us these things not for our amusement but because she wants us to benefit from the example. We must learn, she will remind us with a judicious nod of her head, that the hostess cannot leave her place at table until those around her are at their ease. Her own wishes, and those of her daughters, must be placed second to the needs of others.

The darkness is so intense it seems to be alive. I think of the silver candelabra, drawing those seated round the table into a circle of light. A floorboard creaks and I turn toward the sound.

"Mother?" I whisper.

Your hand is on my arm. I have forgotten you in my musings. I pull back the bedclothes and make room for you. We lie shoulder to shoulder, comforted by each other's presence. You clear your throat and begin.

"Mrs. Dilke," you say in your storytelling voice, "was most surprised one morning to discover that the family had run out of eggs." I settle back on my pillow and let your words weave their spell. Soon I have forgotten the darkness and Mother's broken promise. I am caught up in your world of make-believe. I fall asleep dreaming of hobgoblins and golden hens and eggs fried for breakfast with plenty of frizzle.

"Is she reading it?"

I stand by the window that allows us to see into the drawing room from the conservatory where we work. Mother is in her armchair, the latest copy of our newspaper on the table beside her. She has a letter in her hand and I can tell from the movement of her lips that she is reading parts of it aloud to Father. He is in the armchair next to her and appears engrossed in his book. You are crouching on the floor beside me, your hands pulling nervously at a cushion. Your agitation surprises me. The newspaper is something we have compiled for fun. I peer through the window.

"She's finishing her letter, folding it back into its envelope."

"And has she picked up the newspaper?"

I stare at Mother. She has leaned her head back against the chair rest and closed her eyes. I watch her motionless for a few moments. You pummel the cushion in desperation. I can bear your anxiety no longer.

"Yes," I lie. "She's opening it now."

"Can you see what she's reading? Is it my piece about the pond? Does it make her laugh? What's the expression on her face?"

I turn back to the window. Mother still has her head resting against her chair. I watch her rouse herself, pick up the newspaper, glance at its headline, then let it fall unopened on her lap. I cannot tell you what I see.

"She loves it," I say. "She turned straight to your story and now she's laughing her head off." I pull the curtain firmly across the window and turn away.

You smile as if what I have told you is the most important thing in the world.

It is our ritual. You sit on the bathroom stool, a towel wrapped loosely round your shoulders. I choose lily of the valley and rose water from the shelf and stand behind you. I pour a little of the rose water into my palm and leave it for a moment to warm. Your shoulders are smooth under my fingers. I work my hands down your back, watching your skin undulate to my touch. You lay your head on my chest and as I look down I see the curl of your lashes against your cheek. I knead the soft flesh of your arms as if it is dough.

"Go on," I nudge you gently, "carry on with the story."

The garden is divided by hedges into a sequence of flower beds and lawns. A pocket paradise, Father calls it. We are on the terrace playing cricket. It is my turn to bat. You throw the ball into a high arch and as I wait for it to descend you suddenly abandon your post and start to run, shouting to Thoby and Adrian to follow you. I stand stock still watching the ball, then, prompted by the flare in your eyes, begin to run too. We arrive breathless and excited at the thickets of gooseberries and currants that grow at the back of the vegetable plot. It is only then that I hear Father. You put your finger to your lips, defying us to answer. You march toward the old fountain, bawling a poem at the top of your voice to drown him out. We fall in behind you, obedient soldiers. We are almost at the cracked stone basin when Father catches up with us. He questions you

11

first. You stare him straight in the eye and tell him that you did not hear his call. Your conviction astounds me. Then you swing round and we read clearly your command to lie. Thoby, whose eyes never leave you, shakes his head when Father asks him and is rewarded with your smile. Adrian, delighted to be included in the game, giggles and refuses to speak. It is left to me to bear the brunt of Father's fury.

"Did you not hear me?" Father's cheeks are flushed from the exertion of chasing us across the garden. There is a glare of thunder in his eyes. You watch me intently for a moment. I gaze at the grass.

"Yes, Father," I begin, "we did hear you. We are very sorry we disobeyed you."

The look you turn on me is one of unmitigated scorn.

You are sitting on my bed, my amethyst necklace threaded through your fingers. You hold the stones up to the light.

"This one," you say, as if the beads are a rosary, "is for Mother." I gaze at the jewel's violet sparkle. "Mother who loves the beautiful Nessa more than she has time to say." Your words hit home and I grasp for the necklace. You swing it out of reach and continue your litany unperturbed. "Nessa the bountiful, Nessa the good. If only Mother wasn't so busy." Your tone is artful, wheedling, malicious. "Shall we see who else loves our sister?"

You dangle the beads and your voice tails to a seductive murmur.

"Ah, now who have we here? A poor, orphaned goat, bleating most piteously for her dolphin mother. Someone who would rather Ness didn't scold quite so much, someone who wishes Ness would stop drawing and put her lovely arms round her and pet her."

I know where you are heading and try again for the necklace. You jump off the bed and dart to the window. Before I can say anything, you have climbed onto the ledge, the beads swaying from your fingers.

"Goats are good at climbing, remember. And at leaping." I watch you measure the distance to the chair, and I dart to the window to stop you. You laugh as I catch you round your waist. Your weight drags us to the floor. You clasp my wrists and let your head fall onto my chest. I feel your lips nuzzle my cheek but I am in no mood to baby you. Eel-like, I twist on top of you and use my shoulder as a clamp. Then I seize your fist and prize the necklace loose.

You wait a week for your revenge. We have been walking in Kensington Gardens and are exhilarated by the gift of a balloon from the old woman who sits at the entrance. As we round the corner into Hyde Park Gate we argue about whether or not we should tell Mother about the gift. Your list of reasons for keeping silent is compelling, and as we hang our coats in the hall I acquiesce in the hiding of the balloon in the chest. We remove several rugs in order to accommodate the balloon, and when, later, Mother finds them in our room I feel obliged to confess.

"Is this true, Virginia?" Mother hates deceitfulness and her tone is stern. You glare at me before you answer.

"What you see before you, Mother," you say, with a spiteful glitter in your eye, "is a devil and a saint!" You take a mock bow then point to me. To my amazement, instead of chastising you, Mother laughs. That evening your phrase is repeated to Father, who claps his hands at your wit. Soon he is calling me "saint" and winking at you. George, Gerald, even Thoby join in the taunt. I feel constrained by your tag but do not know how to retaliate. Any suggestion that you might be a devil seems to slip from everyone's mind.

The first week of July. The trunks are packed ready in the hall. We crowd into the carriage that will take us to the station, our arms full of books, spades, butterfly nets, cricket bats, tins of crayons, straw hats. I sit pushed up against the window. The swallows weave and dip like runaway shuttles against the cerulean blue of the sky. All winter we have waited for this moment.

Inside the train everyone talks at once. We count the stations, straining for a glimpse of the sea. Father sets his books aside and takes hold of Mother's hand.

On holiday in St. Ives we do not keep to our rigid London schedules. Guests come and go according to the dictates of the trains and not the immutable pattern of meal and visiting times we live by at home. Even Father appears released from the relentless burden of work that oppresses him in London, finding time for walks, outings, games. We are given an unprecedented freedom to roam the garden and neighboring beach almost at will. The house is light and airy, the rooms opening out of each other like origami boxes. Somehow Mother makes all the piecemeal arrangements coalesce.

It is here that I come alive. Shut up all year like Persephone, it is as if my reward for the sacrifice, the absence of horizon, is a sudden baptism of light. Like a starved prisoner I drink it in. All summer long I try to bottle the light, store it up, capture it in my sketches, so that I can take it back to London with me and feed on it during the dreary winter months. In St. Ives I am at liberty to draw and paint all day. It is here that I do my first serious exercises, Stella guiding my hand as I discover new shapes to fill the dark.

Thoby looks preposterous in his suit, as if he is trying to impersonate a grownup. Mother tucks a clean handkerchief into his pocket and pulls his collar straight. Then she beckons us forward. We shake hands, conscious of our awkwardness. Father appears at the top of the stairs and adds a final injunction to the leave-taking. We watch Thoby vanish into his carriage and I feel your fingers clutch mine. It is beginning to dawn on both of us that our beloved brother will not be home for some time.

Did we long to follow Thoby to school? It is a complicated question. Part of me yearned to break free from that dark, imprisoning house and discover life for myself, while another part drew back, reluctant to relinquish the familiar template. There is no doubt that his going sealed us even more completely into our pact. We became each other's mirrors, as our lessons and walks marked the contours of a day in which we were required to depend largely on ourselves. We spent hours alone together in the small conservatory, you reading aloud while I sketched, hours open-eyed in our adjacent beds at night, your tales the only glow in the unremitting black. To this day, when I read it is your voice and not mine that I hear, your pitch inflecting the thoughts that beat in my head as I drift off to sleep.

There was an arrogance in our complicity. We had no external reference but each other, no guide to direct us, no check on our imaginings and delusions. We were pitiless with the failings of others. Metamorphosed in the mill of your descriptive genius, the weaknesses and foibles of those around us became props to shore up our own faltering self-images.

You were the one with words. You were the one who knew how to take an event and describe it so that its essence was revealed. I do not have your talents. If you were here you would know how to tell this tale. You would find a way of penetrating to the truth and enclosing what you found in words of such poetry that one's heart would sing, even as it wept.

Easter. We walk through the park as usual, stopping to gaze at the crocuses that erupt like lava from the winter-brown crust of the flower borders. On the path by the pond Mrs. Redgrave comes toward us in her bath chair, looking, you say, like something from the museum that has not been successfully preserved. As we enter the hall Miss Mills nods at us from her rostrum, her crucifix gleaming against the slate gray of her dress. The rest of the girls assemble and Miss Mills appeals for our attention.

"Who can tell me what day it is?" There is a timorousness in her voice, a plea to be listened to and liked, which you find infuriating. You mutter something under your breath. Julia Martin steps forward.

"Please, Miss Mills, it's Easter Friday."

Miss Mills beams and looks up at the ceiling, as if she is communicating with a higher power.

"Exactly. The day our dear Lord died on the cross. Good Friday."

"Good?" I hear you snort with derision. You draw a question mark in the dust with your toe.

"Who is that talking?" When she realizes it is you, Miss Mills takes on the air of a beleaguered captain who knows from past experience that this will be a difficult skirmish. "What is it, Virginia?"

Her lips are set in a line of firm resolution. Something in her expression fans your sense of the ridiculous, and you stuff your cuff in your mouth to stifle your laugh. In a moment I am seized too, shoulders twitching as I try to conceal my mirth. We stand together, heads bowed, allies against the preposterousness of the world.

We were trained to be ladies. How was it you put it once? We learned to venerate the angel of virtue, whose selflessness was such that she had no requirements of her own. She was paraded constantly before us, our goal and unrelenting goad. She shamed us when we failed to imitate her, stood in the way of any ambitions we might have. Little wonder, then, that you murdered her, stabbed the point of your pen in her perfect, impossible breast.

It is four o'clock. I pause at the entrance to the drawing room and pull my skirt straight. Father glowers as I enter. I notice a stain of paint on my hand and tuck it behind my back. I seat myself on the couch next to Mother. A knock on the door announces the first guest. We begin our familiar routine.

We are mechanical figures, you and I, controlled by an invisible puppeteer. We listen and observe, saying only enough to keep the ball of conversation lopping backward and forward across the table. We are its reluctant guardians, required to keep it always in motion, suppressing any desires we might have to send it spinning out of orbit or to allow it to settle for a moment at rest. We must pat it to the shy young woman in the corner, judging our stroke so that it will land gently enough to encourage her to raise her racket and participate in the game. We must sequester it away from the monopoly of our aunts batting it conspiratorially between them, somehow prevent the young men sitting with Father from stealing it to show off their learning.

You are better at it than I am. You become a mistress of disguise. I am astonished, as I listen to you, at the way you weave your barbs into a fabric of such loveliness that your interlocutor is left wondering whether it is a compliment or an insult you intend. I lack your subtlety and skill.

You were to record, later, the impact that tea-table training had on your writing, so that you never felt able to give yourself free rein. You had words at your disposal nevertheless, and you found a way to survive. For me it was different. I had to fish in precisely that area of myself where I felt most ill at ease. I was always running out of things to say, straying into territories I knew were forbidden and where I exposed myself to censure, or coming aground on the banks of an unstoppable pause. Increasingly, I copied Mother, adopting her silent attentiveness as my costume for those apprenticeship afternoons.

We learned even as we despised. Young, earnest, eager to please, we were like fledgling birds watching for the clues that would enable us to fly. We caught occasional glimpses of the dancing kite tails of our lives in the space ahead of us, and our hearts quickened in response. We longed to take the leap that would allow us to chase after them, yet we clung to the safety of our nest.

You walk along the bank searching for stones to fill your pockets. I think of you that day, staring into the fast-flowing river, the still leafless branches of the trees etched against the ghostly gray of the sky. I try to picture what went on inside your head.

Did you remember me, Leonard, the children, as you left your stick on the bank and strode out into the swirling water, or were all your thoughts bent on escaping what you could no longer bear to endure?

You see, even after all these years, I wonder if you really loved me.

2

IT IS STELLA WHO WAKES US. THE LIGHT FROM HER candle throws ghastly shadows on the wall. I know at once that it is serious. I sit up in bed, pulling my dressing gown round my shoulders, and slip my feet into my shoes. You wrap yourself in a shawl, shivering with the cold. When we are ready we follow Stella to Mother's room. At the doorway we hold hands. Father is in a chair by the bed, his head buried in his palms. Dr. Seton is standing by the window, talking to George and Gerald. Two nurses arrange Mother's pillows. There is a hush as we enter the room. We stay close to Stella, who puts her arm round our shoulders. George comes forward and tells us we must each kiss Mother in turn. He holds out his hand to Adrian and leads him to Mother's side. I see Adrian stoop to kiss Mother's cheek, clinging to George's fingers. As George takes you to the bed Mother's eyes flick open. She looks at you calmly for a moment. Then her eyes close again.

Now it is my turn. I bend down to kiss Mother's forehead and hear the awful drag of her breathing. I need her to speak to me. I need her to explain what is happening. I need her to tell me she loves me. Her eyes remain resolutely closed. I feel George's hand on my arm and allow him to lead me away.

I sit staring at the floor. I cannot bear to look at the bed. I can hear the birds singing outside the window. Opposite me is Mother's dressing table; I look at her jewelry box, her photographs, her notebook and pen. The mirror is set at an angle and in it I can see Mother's reflection. Her face is almost translucent in the half-light. I study her as if she is a painting, noting the pallor of her skin, the way the hair parts over her brow. I try to decide how I would draw her. There are dark shadows over the eye sockets, and the bow of the upper lip is so pronounced that the lower lip seems almost to disappear into it.

I am conscious of the room growing brighter. Still staring into the mirror, I watch Dr. Seton lift Mother's wrist and take her pulse. He nods, and settles her arm back by her side. Father lets out a great, raging howl.

I flee from the room.

We huddle in the drawing room, uncertain how to continue. We are like figures from which all form, all color, all life has drained out. The curtains are pulled against the chill spring light. George sits by the fireplace, weeping. Gerald stares dumbly at his hands. Above us, we can hear Father's wild sobs. Stella comes into the room, carrying a jug of warm milk and a bottle of brandy. You gaze into the fire, your eyes vacant. What has happened is beyond our understanding.

We sip the warm milk. Already the thought is beginning to dawn on me that Mother's death could have been prevented. I picture Dr. Seton, always in a hurry, leaving the care of his patient to the nurses. I remember Father, wearing Mother out with his perpetual demands. You caught him perfectly in your novel, when you described his famished beak draining her energy dry. His cries will not reach her now.

Aunt Mary's face is screwed into an imitation of misery. She holds out her hand and, when I shake it, crushes me unwillingly to her breast. Her jet beads cut into my cheek.

"You poor darling," she says, rolling her eyes heavenward. She smells of camphor and cold cream. She spies Ellen coming down the stairs and releases me to remove her coat. Then she ushers me into the drawing room.

"I want you to promise," she begins, settling herself in the chair by the fire, "I want you to promise that it is me you will come to if you have any little question or problem." She leans herself back more comfortably against the cushions. "Now, let us talk about your lessons. Who is supervising your piano playing? I know the most marvelous tutor who would be only too delighted to instruct you. I hope you are not still seeing that dreadful Mrs. Watts."

It was Sargent, years later at the Royal Academy, who said he found my paintings too gray. Yet the one that seems to me to most closely evoke this time is anything but somber. There is a black line running diagonally across it, dividing the almost monotone blue of the upper part from the murky whiteness of the central space. I had the sand and sea in my eyes as I worked on it, but as I look at it now what I see is something else. The blue is separated so completely from the white that it is as if the painting captures two different worlds. At the front, in the left-hand corner, set against the barren whiteness, is a yellow-brown triangle, a rock, perhaps. Two figures sit in its shadow.

One is bigger than the other and the clothes and pose suggest a mother and child. The figures are viewed from behind and all we see of the mother is the back of her coat and the brim and crown of her hat. The child is similarly attired, though there is an alertness in the tilt of the hat that is entirely absent from the mother's outline. The abstractness of the form suggests vacancy, as if the mother's vital presence has somehow been extinguished. Opposite the pair, on the right, near the boundary line, is a large, luminous shape. Before it stands a woman dressed in blue, her long hair hanging down her back. At her feet a group of children squat, engrossed in play. I think of the bathing hut Mother used to change in, but as I look again it is not this I see. What dominates as I look at the picture today is the ethereal radiance of this lone object. It is as if the woman is devoured by its brilliance. There is the bare expanse on which the children focus their attention, while the mother slips into unmitigated blue. Yet I never imagined Mother in heaven.

"Do you miss her?" I know as soon as I have spoken that my question is a mistake. Stella bows her head over her sewing, trying to hide her distress. I want to claw my words back, undo the hurt they have caused. Since Mother's death Stella has become indispensable to me and I would do anything to avoid giving her pain. I know how tired she is. I hear her at night, getting up to attend to Father, soothing his grief-stricken outbursts. It is Stella who manages the household now. I realize that the angle of her neck as she leans over her sewing is an exact replica of the way Mother sat.

"Ginia called out in her sleep again last night." The ploy works. Stella lifts her head and looks at me.

"Were you able to make out any of what she was saying?"

"Not very much."

"I will speak to Dr. Seton again." Stella's concern is clear. I have no choice but to continue.

"I think she said 'Stand up straight, little goat.'" We are two mothers, joined in solicitude for our charge.

"I wonder what she meant." Stella reaches for the scissors and snips the end of her thread. She holds her shirt up to inspect it.

"I'm relieved Father has agreed that Adrian should not go away to school. I don't think he would stand it." She folds the shirt neatly and picks up the next garment on the pile.

"And what about you, Nessa? How are you getting on with your drawing? I liked your picture of the lilies." I blush with pleasure. The collar I am working on suddenly seems aureoled with light. I think of the lilies, the intricate tracery of their petals, their solid, trumpet-like shapes. For the first time in weeks I sense a glimmer of hope.

You are standing on the windowsill, your arms stretched out like an avenging angel. You stare at me as I come toward you. You shriek that if I advance any closer you will hurl yourself through the windowpane. Your hand clutches for something to smash the glass. On the floor there are the remains of a plate you have flung at the wall. Your shrieking stops and I see your body tremble. Slowly, tenderly, you let me lead you to your bed.

I sketch an apple that Stella has left on the table. You are lying face down and appear to be asleep. Every now and then I hear you whimper. You have not eaten for two days. The light streams through the window, casting bars of shadow on the floor.

"It will dissolve us all." I stop drawing and look up. You have raised yourself onto your elbows and are gazing at the light flooding onto your pillow.

"Would you like me to close the curtains?" My voice is a whisper. These are your first distinct words for some time.

"Yes."

I stand up and pull the curtains to, then come round to the side of your bed. You turn and face me.

"She told me to stand up straight." You say the words as if they are a question to which you despair of ever being able to find an answer.

"Do you think the birds were singing for her?"

I sit on the bed and stroke your hair. You are as vulnerable in my arms as a child.

Three days a week I escape. Oh, the delirious happiness of banging the front door behind me and launching into the teeming bustle of the streets! The air fans my cheek as I cycle along Queen's Gate. I tear past strolling couples, nannies with their charges, gray-suited men on their way to work, and feel as if I have a purpose in life.

The desks are arranged in a semicircle. Set on a pillar in their midst is a marble bust. Mr. Cope, the drawing master, stops at each of our desks in turn, looking, offering advice, occasionally altering a line. There is a concentrated quiet as we contemplate the object before us. What we are attempting is not an act of transferal. We are not trying to reproduce the bust. Rather, we are struggling to convey what we see — the figure's relationship to the space around it, the way the light falls and obliterates part of a cheek — and this is infinitely more difficult.

The face is of a Greek goddess — Artemis, perhaps, or Aphrodite. I focus on the jaw and neck, trying to understand the connection between them. Mr. Cope comes and stands behind me. He watches but does not interfere. He knows that this is something I must do for myself and leaves me to battle on alone.

I immerse myself in the conundrum of my picture. I grapple with space and form, light and dark, contour and texture. In the process I forget your pain and Father's misery and Stella's cares.

The hands on the clock move forward. At last I stand back and consider my work. I survey the arch of the nose, the angle of the mouth, the slope of the throat and shoulders. I nod. I am pleased with what I have achieved. I have given my goddess life.

The light from the stained-glass window casts dancing oblongs of color on the stone floor of the church. Everywhere I look I see faces straining for a glimpse of the bride. Jack is already at the altar. We wait with Stella in the vestibule, trying to quell Father's protests that he is being abandoned, and watch for the vicar's signal. At last the organ begins its march and we make our way down the aisle.

I cannot take my eyes off Stella. There is something different about her. I look at her walking ahead of me on Father's arm, nodding to the assembled guests, and search for the words to describe her. She is like a sleepwalker who has been woken from her trance. As she takes her place next to Jack at the altar, she is no longer a girl bowed down by duty but a woman transformed. In her vows I hear the inklings of a promise: life can continue without Mother.

~

The bird is so lifelike I gasp. I pull the sketchbook toward me and study the picture. I take in the accuracy of the outline, the intricate shading of the feathers, the perfectly observed detail of eye and beak and claw. Sensing my admiration, Thoby turns the page, and I see a series of smaller drawings of the same bird.

"These are the ones I started with. I knew what I wanted but somehow it was easier to begin by trying out a number of angles." I understand exactly what Thoby means and nod.

"Yes. I often find that it's as I'm drawing that I discover how I'm going to do it. Even if I know exactly what it is I want. It's as if I have to discard all the other options first." Thoby does not reply but instead points to another of his sketches. This one is of a robin, its red breast picked out in crayon.

"I had a time of it here. Couldn't get the color right."

"Crayons are hard," I say sympathetically.

"Hard, yes — but it's the difficulty that makes it exciting! Nature is so varied."

I move closer to the candlelight. The torment of the past months seems to disappear in the darkness that surrounds us. Thoby's arm is round my shoulder, and as I lean into his warmth I can feel his heart beating. I should like this moment to last forever.

A door slams somewhere in the house and I hear footsteps in the hall. Your face appears in the doorway.

"So there you are!" You do nothing to disguise your annoyance. "I've been looking for you everywhere. What are you doing?" You approach the table and peer at the robin.

"Oh, drawings," you say.

I feel Thoby pull away.

"I'm glad to find you, anyway. I've been rereading *Antony*

and Cleopatra." You stare pointedly at Thoby. "Really, I don't understand what you mean about Shakespeare's women being such glorious creatures. It seems to me they are cut out with a pair of scissors. Not so much actual women as a man's tailored view of how women should be."

Your words have the effect you intend. Thoby turns on you.

"Nonsense!" His eyes brim with delight at the prospect of an intellectual duel. "That's absolutely not what they are."

"Come now," you goad, "you'll have to prove your point better than that. I give you they talk divinely. I was looking at Cleopatra's dream of Antony and it sent shivers down my spine. That still doesn't make them real, though."

I have stopped listening. I walk to the window. All I can see are your reflections. I press my forehead to the glass and let your words run on, as if they are no more consequential than the raindrops I watch coursing down the pane. I know that for the rest of the evening you will monopolize Thoby. You will move from Shakespeare to the Greeks then on to the Romantics, and I will be more firmly excluded with each transition. Thoby's sketchbook will lie unopened between you. I wait until my forehead is as cold as the glass then leave the room. Neither of you notice as I pull the door closed behind me.

The letter sits in its envelope, radiating friendliness. I butter my toast and mull over Margery's words. Her decision to leave painting aside for a while in order to improve her drawing interests me. I think of Cope's insistence on the importance of line and wonder if I should do the same. Suddenly I want to be at my easel. You and Adrian are having one of your arguments and I know that if I stay I will be drawn in. I eat my toast and push back my chair. You look up. You have been so engrossed in your attack on Adrian that you have not noticed my letter. You stare at it.

"A letter! Who is it from?" You hold out your hand. I hesistate.

"It's from Margery." I do not want to tell you even this much.

"Margery! And what is her crisis? I suppose she writes it at great length and with much misspelling. I never met anyone who mangles the English language with such constancy. She merits a prize!" I say nothing. Adrian concentrates on his breakfast, glad to be free of your stranglehold at last.

"Do let's hear it. I could do with some entertainment."

Gerald enters the dining room. He sits on the empty chair opposite Adrian and gives him a wan smile. He still cannot forgive Adrian, Mother's youngest child, for being her favorite. He has overheard your remark and looks at you inquisitively.

"What's all this about entertainment?"

"Nessa has a missive from the divine Margery," you say coolly. "And we are itching to hear of her latest calamity."

"Margery?" Gerald's brow furrows as he tries to place her.

"Snowden," you prompt.

"Oh, one of the painters. Yes, by all means let's hear what she has to say. Is there any marmalade?"

You have Gerald on board. I stare miserably at my envelope.

"It's private," I say timidly.

"All the more reason. Private always means something delicious. Come on, let's have it."

I ignore you. I pass Gerald the marmalade. Then I take the envelope and stand up. To my annoyance you follow me out of the room.

30

"Ness?" Your tone now is pleading. I know I have to speak.

"Margery has written to *me*. I don't think I should let you read what she says." You flinch. You do not like me keeping secrets.

"Is she unwell?" You sound concerned but I am suspicious it is another of your ruses. I determine to stand firm.

"She is perfectly well. She simply wishes to tell me a decision she has come to about painting." I know as soon as I say this that it is a mistake. It is a reminder of another domain we do not share.

"You are being unfair. I show you all my letters."

"Perhaps it's time we stopped. Perhaps it's time we had interests and friendships outside the family."

You stare at me. A new thought forms in your eyes.

"But Margery? She's hardly your equal, Ness. She's one of those women who blunders through life, straining to keep pace with those she'd like to copy. She's a drain on you."

I can think of no answer to your jealousy and turn away.

"Don't go!" I hear the panic in your voice but I dare not give in. If I let you read the letter you will ridicule and demolish it until there is nothing left to threaten you. I push the envelope into my sleeve and head upstairs.

"It's the fact that she must stand." Aunt Minna puts her cup down on the table. Her starched collar crackles as she reaches for the pot. "Another for you, Leslie?"

Father's only response is a grunt. For the past half-hour he has sat staring into the empty space ahead of him, his silence broken only by the occasional groan. Aunt Minna has not yet abandoned her aim of trying to cheer him and interprets his grunt as a yes.

31

"Pass me your father's cup, will you, Virginia? There's a dear."

You glare at Aunt Minna and I see that you have taken her silly observation to heart. Aunt Minna prattles on.

"Writing seems to me a much better activity for a woman. The body is supported, and as long as one makes sure to sit up straight there is no pressure on the back. I can't think it can be good for Vanessa to have to stand all day before an easel. Have you thought, dear, of the impact on your posture?"

I ignore Aunt Minna. I know what she says is kindly meant. I watch you pick up Father's cup and pass it to her. There is no mistaking the look of fury on your face.

Only later do I realize the extent of your anger. For your birthday you ask Father for a lectern so that you can write standing up. You will not allow that mine is the more difficult art.

It is late when I come into our room. I have been trying to finish a picture, and in my absorption I have forgotten the time. Though I saw you go up to bed I do not think you will be asleep. I decide to tell you about the problems I have been struggling with in my composition.

As I push open the door the room is in darkness. I feel my way toward your bed, letting my eyes accustom themselves to the black. As I get closer I see an unexpected shape. To my astonishment I realize it is George. He jumps up at once.

"Here you are at last, Nessa. I was just keeping Ginny company." His voice is pinched and tight, as if he is fighting to control his breath.

"Well, I shall leave you to sleep. Goodnight, dear sisters. How I envy you your beds pushed so closely together. That must be a great comfort to you both." I hear the squeak of his shoes as he makes his way to the door.

I go over to you. You are lying with your face buried in your arms. A terrible thought crosses my mind.

"He didn't — you know . . ." Your answer is so faint that I must bend over you to catch it.

"No. No. Nothing like that." I hear the tremor in your voice.

"Does George come in here often when I'm downstairs?" Your response is a wild sob.

The spider sits motionless in its web. It is outside the window and raindrops have collected on its sticky threads. They glitter as they catch the light. The wind gusts across the garden at an alarming rate. Suddenly there is a great crack. A branch from one of the trees tears free. I glance at the web. The spider is still there, the threads intact. I marvel at their tenacity. They look as if a breath could dislodge them, yet they hold while the oak tree falls.

I come into the drawing room, conscious of the image I create. I am swathed in white voile overlaid with black and silver sequins that fissure into tiny rainbows in the light. I have amethysts and opals round my neck and my hair is pinned with enamel butterflies. I am taut with anticipation. George is standing by the fireplace and turns toward me as I enter the room. He raises his eyeglass and appraises me. There is no difference between this gesture and his scrutiny of the Arab mare he has bought for my daily rides. I look to you for protection. You are sitting next to Father, reading. I see from your eyes as you lift them from your page that I am changed.

George does not speak as we drive in the carriage to the party. He leans his head against the rest and smokes his cigar. I look out the window at the necklace of streetlamps. I sense that something momentous is about to occur.

The rooms are ablaze with light. We stand for a moment on the balcony and gaze down at the dancers on the floor below. The couples weave in elegant formations, as brilliant as the butterflies in my hair. I should like to stay and watch them. I should like the opportunity to observe this world before I enter it. George tidies the folds of my dress and clasps my arm.

Several heads turn our way as we are announced. George keeps a firm grip on my elbow. He steers me through the throng of people and stops in front of a hatchet-faced man. He has designs for me.

"Just arrived, Duckworth?" The two men shake hands.

"Mr. Chamberlain, allow me to present my half sister, Miss Vanessa Stephen." I see the hand stretch out toward me. George's hot breath is on the back of my neck, willing me to comply. The hand looms closer, imperious, expectant, impatient. I am insubstantial and ridiculous in my dress. I pray for one of the dancers gliding past to catch hold of me and swirl me away. Miserably I shake the hand. I can think of nothing to say.

We leave early. George helps me into the carriage without a word. I know he is angry. He waits until we are on our way before he erupts.

"Would you like to tell me what that was about? I suppose you think it is amusing to insult people. You do realize who that was?"

I bow my head. The streetlamps are blurred smears in the wet panes of the carriage window.

34

"Your hair was awful, too! Why can't you keep it pinned up? You must learn to use those clips I bought you."

Poor George! My silences were unacceptable in the circles he moved in, but so, paradoxically, was your ability to talk. The night you tried to discuss Plato with the people he had seated around you at dinner was a humiliation for you both. If only he had not staked so much on our success! If only he had left us to find our own way in the social sea into which he cast us, instead of forcing us forward where we foundered, things might have been different. Yet as I think back to that time now I cannot blame him entirely. I suspect we owe something of what we later accomplished to his influence. George's constant haranguing, his perpetual reminders as to our place and obligations, focused what might have remained vague longings for an alternative.

If this were a work of fiction, instead of an attempt to discern the truth, then Stella's death, coming so soon after Mother's, would seem like malicious overload on the writer's part. Stella's return from her honeymoon, thin and desperately ill, tolled a death knell for our hope that life might offer fresh chances. It was as if the awakening we had witnessed the day of her marriage had to be paid for. She had filled the void Mother left behind her only to be stolen from us in turn. We clung to each other as her life slipped away, and learned that happiness is fleeting.

The noose of domesticity draws round me. No one tells me I must stand on the steps each morning and wave Adrian off to school, or that I must carry Father's hot milk to him at night, but I sense that if I do not do these things the great lumbering

35

motion of the household will grind to a halt. I dare not let myself think about Stella. If I try to sleep, terrifying images crowd around me. My only refuge is my work. I paint until I am so tired I can scarcely hold my brush. Then I lie down and force myself to continue my picture in my head.

The only person I wish to see is Stella's husband, Jack. He visits most evenings and we sit together in the drawing room. I sew in Mother's chair while he tells me about his day. I like to feel him watching me.

"You look tired, Nessa. I'm certain you're doing too much," he says one evening. I am not used to being treated with such solicitude.

"I'm worried about Adrian. He has a nasty cut on his leg. I sometimes think that if there were an open field with only one obstacle in it Adrian would find it and hurt himself on it. Are all children so accident-prone?" It is unlike me to confide so much. Jack's hand reaches out and gently clasps mine.

"You should not be carrying all this. Your father places too much responsibility on you. It was the same with Stella." I find I can bear Jack mentioning her name. I let his fingers stroke mine.

I wait for Jack's visits. Directly after dinner I go upstairs and tidy my hair. I loop it behind my ears then gather it in a bunch. Mother wore her hair coiled at her neck whereas Stella piled hers higher on her head. I experiment with both styles. You watch me from your bed, frowning. You sense that I am doing this for Jack and you do not like it. One evening, as I try a brooch at my throat, you can restrain yourself no longer.

"He won't notice! Why are you wasting your time on him?" You sound like a petulant child. Suddenly you burst out laughing.

"D-d-d-dearest d-d-do sit d-d-down and r-r-rest." I smart at your parody of Jack's stammer. Instead of joining in your joke I should like to slap you. I push past you, letting my silence express my displeasure.

The letter I receive from Aunt Mary advising me to stop seeing Jack is so ridiculous I want to burn it. Instead, I carry it into the dining room and fling it on the breakfast table. Thoby, still at home for the holidays, sees.

"What's the matter, Nessa? You look as if you've been struck by lightning."

"I have. I've just opened this letter from Aunt Mary, who thinks it her business to decide who my friends should be."

George, still yawning in his dressing gown, stretches lazily.

"If she means Jack then I have to say I agree. After all, it would be an illegal match. A man cannot marry his deceased wife's sister."

I am appalled. My feelings for Jack have never taken such a definite form. I look at Thoby to rescue me.

"George is right, you know. Best to stop seeing Jack." This time, the lightning strike is real. In my agitation, I let my knife slide to the floor. You stoop to retrieve it.

"Poppycock! If that's what the law says then the law needs to be changed. It's hardly incest." You look coolly at George, taunting him to take up your bait. Thoby answers.

"All the same, I think you should listen to Aunt Mary. She means well, and it's true that if Nessa did try to marry Jack it would create the most awful stink."

"I beg your pardon. Since when did Aunt Mary mean well?" The fierceness of your support surprises me. "Aunt Mary has never given a moment's thought to Nessa's happiness. All she was thinking about when she wrote that letter was her own

37

reputation. Actually I'm rather sorry Stella didn't have more husbands. Perhaps, if we had each married one, we could both have broken the law." You slip the knife back into my hand with a wink.

Violet comes to visit. Her tall figure, exaggerated by her ramshackle clothes, hurries to greet us. As she holds out her arms I cannot help remembering that it was Stella who first introduced us. Violet stops in the hallway and retrieves a paper from her bag. I see that it is something you have written. She whispers as she presses it into your hand. I can tell by your face that she has praised you.

We go into the drawing room and settle round the fire. You sit at Violet's feet, your back resting against her legs. She wastes no time in explaining the reason for her visit.

"I have been thinking about the two of you, marooned in this gloomy house. I'm sure the best thing for you would be to get away. I've talked it over with Ozzie. Why don't the pair of you come and stay with me? At least for a while, until you find your feet. I could look after you."

I watch Violet's hand reach down and caress your hair. You lay your head in her lap and close your eyes. My mind races to thoughts of Adrian, Father, Thoby. It is as if I have spoken aloud.

"I know you're worried about Adrian, but neither of you can mother him. Besides, with the two of you gone, the men will have to look after themselves."

I smile in spite of myself at the thought of Father coping.

"Well, my dears, it's entirely up to you. I'm sure it would do you both good. We could have a jolly time together."

Later that night, I think over Violet's plan. The prospect of relinquishing the household duties is an appealing one.

"Billy. Are you asleep? Shall we go to Violet's?"

I hear you stir in the darkness.

"It's an absurd idea! Who would look after Father? And there's Adrian to consider!" Something in your tone rings false.

"I was wondering if we might ask Aunt Caroline to come."

"Aunt Caroline! You know how she irritates Father! I'd much rather things went on as they are. After all, I can see Violet whenever I like."

I do not press the point home. I am not certain enough to try to win you round. I lie back on my pillow and remember the look on your face as you let Violet stroke your hair. A new thought dawns on me.

"I don't believe you. I think you want to keep Violet to yourself!"

"Come."

The door, as it opens, reveals a deluge of papers. The floor is strewn with discarded pages covered in Father's handwriting. The curtains are half-drawn against the light, and it takes my eyes a few moments to adjust to the semidarkness. Father is behind his desk, surrounded by books. There are books lining the shelves on the wall behind him, books lying open in front of him, books stacked in precarious towers at his feet. He looks up as I enter.

"The accounts, Father."

I hold out the ledger. He takes it from me and scowls. His eyebrows knit together as his finger traces the lists of figures it has taken me many hours to construct. His finger stops at one of the entries.

"What's this? Strawberries! You allowed Sophie to order strawberries in May!" Father raises his eyes from the offending item, javelins of suspicion. I open my mouth to explain. I want to tell him about the look that comes across Sophie's face if I try to contradict her. I want to confess my lack of experience. I want to ask for his help. His eyes have already turned back to the page.

"Salmon! Do you mean to tell me that the fish we ate Tuesday last was salmon? Look at the price, girl! Why this extravagance? Would whiting not have sufficed?" I stare at the floor. I think of the ivy curtaining the kitchen window and its green tinge on Sophie's cheek as she quashed my protests about the fish. My silence seems to goad Father on.

"You stand there like a block of stone! Do you have nothing to say to me?"

I think of the gash in your coat, the money I must conjure for sanitary towels and turps. I can enter none of these things in the rigid grid Father has devised.

"Do you wish to ruin me?" Father slams the book shut and pushes it toward me. I think of how he would behave, rationally, man to man, if it were George or Thoby presenting the accounts instead of me.

"Can you not imagine what it is like for me now? Have you no pity?" It is bearing down on me, Father's beak. I feel it ripping into my flesh, ravenous for sympathy.

Finally I am released. I go out onto the landing bowed down by my failure. You are sitting on the bottom stair. I can tell from your expression that you have been listening to our exchange. Your eyes signal your compassion, your powerlessness to help.

"Damn him!" I burst out.

I realize from the tapering light in your eyes that I have gone too far. You look away. You are only a partial accomplice. I sense from the set of your shoulders, a sudden movement of your arm, that though you acknowledge Father's tyranny you love him still.

I lift my head from my page and try to peer back through the alleys of the past. It seems extraordinary to me now that we survived that time. Only to you could I confess some of what I felt. Only you shared my dream. Secretly, but with increasing resolve, we sketched out a life where we were each free to pursue our chosen art.

Neither of us realized how much we sacrificed in the process. We placated each other by exaggerating our differences, renouncing all claim to the other's field. I, always less skillful with words than you, relinquished them to you entirely. I took painting for myself.

3

SOMETIMES I STAB FATHER, SOMETIMES I SMOTHER him with his pillow, sometimes it is the lethal mix of medicines I pour from the vials on his bedside table that kills him. Though there are variations in my method, the dream always takes the same form. I am in the hall, the front door open before me, when I hear Father's voice. I stand for a moment in the doorway and feel the warmth of the sun on my face. There is a child on the pavement opposite, running headlong from the clutches of its nurse. I consider joining the child in its dash for freedom, slamming the door on Father's tremulous call. I weigh my hat in my hands. The child and nurse pass from view. I close the front door and watch the light disappear. Then I make my way up the stairs to Father's room. At his door I pause and look about me. I do not want anyone to witness what I am about to do. Father's head swivels toward me as I go in. I kill him quickly, effortlessly. I do it without volition and he makes no attempt to resist. It is as if a pact is being played out between us. I walk to the window, pull open the curtains, and let the light flood in. Then I wake up.

We stand together, watching the bearers lower Father into the frozen ground. His cancer has taken him at last. I realize from the look in your eyes that you are determined to remember him as finer than he was, that you will erase from your memory all his petty tyrannies, his appeals for our sympathy. I find it preposterous that you should have such feelings now that we are finally free. Despite your warning glances I refuse to cry. I take the shovel Thoby passes me and let the soil cascade into Father's grave.

"The king," you say suddenly, "stopped outside your window and told you the whole dirty tale."

I look up in surprise from my chair. You point an accusing finger at me.

"There," you shout, leaping out of bed, "there is the culprit. Seize her!" I do not know for whom your words are intended but they have the effect of bringing the nurse running into the room. She puts a restraining arm round you and coaxes you back to bed. She signals that it would be better if I left.

I stop writing to watch the birds pecking at the bacon rinds Grace has flung on the lawn. I can hear their rapid seesaws of sound even though the window is closed. They sang in Greek, you explained, as I left you to the care of your nurse, though there was no mistaking their meaning.

In a way I do not fully understand, I think your madness spared me. As I listened to your wild rantings my mind took refuge in ordinary things: a shaft of sunlight on your dressing table, clouds chasing each other across the sky. It was as if your visions stood in for my own feelings, enabling me to go on with my life.

That year, we went to Cornwall on our own. The weather was glorious, I remember, and Thoby, Adrian, and I roamed the coastal paths for miles. You refused to come walking with us. Once the sea was so wild that I took off my shoes and stockings and strode out into the foamy spray. The wind tore at my hair and my skirt billowed round me and I felt as I looked at the surging torrents as if I could accomplish anything. We returned from our walk to find you cloistered in the sitting room, poring over one of Father's books. You had pulled the curtains half-shut. Thoby and Adrian fell silent as we entered the gloomy interior.

"What's that you're reading, Ginny?" You lift the book high enough for me to see that it is Hardy's elegies.

"The waves were heavenly. You should have come with us." It is Thoby now who takes up the fray. He settles himself on the sofa, his skin radiant from the sun.

"Yes, we thought we might get a boat and go to the Godrevy lighthouse tomorrow." Thoby's high spirits have made Adrian bold. You sit resolutely silent, your book held before you like a sneer. At last Thoby flings his feet off the sofa and stands up.

"I'm going to see what's happening with lunch. I could eat a horse!" He launches a cushion at Adrian and the pair race each other out of the room. I linger for a moment, consumed with guilt. It is only when I get to the door that I hear your voice.

"There'll be no going to the lighthouse tomorrow. It's forecast rain."

༄

Paris. The daring simplicity of Manet. Surfaces struck as planes of color — maroon, lemon, pale blue. Light allowed to infuse the painting so the essence of the subject is caught.

The bar curves out from the wall, forming a centerpiece to the room. At one end there is a large jug of flowers, scarlet snapdragons, purple zinnias, great white peonies with blooms the size of saucers, fronds of lacy gypsophila, dusky-pink poppies, long-stemmed yellow daisies. All along the bar are high wooden stools, many of them occupied. The café owner stands behind the bar, rinsing glasses under a tap. He is a broad-chested man with a shock of black hair, and wears a grease-smeared white apron round his waist. Behind him there are shelves stacked with bottles, packets of cigarettes, jars of tobacco, plates. A waiter weaves among the tables, his tray held high above his head. Everywhere is the sound of eager, animated conversation.

Thoby sits with his back pressed against the window. His thick hair flops over his forehead. He has his arms folded across his chest and surveys the scene before him with evident delight. The waiter appears and sets a basket of bread and a carafe of red wine down on our table. Clive, who has been entertaining us with an account of his attempts to consult a government archive, stops talking and reaches for a piece of bread. He takes a bite and chews it thoughtfully.

"What is it about French bread?" He holds the slice up as if it is an object of veneration. "How is it that something so ordinary can taste so delicious when eaten in convivial surroundings?" He beams at us, a broad conspiratorial grin. His skin is almost white against the rich auburn of his hair.

"There isn't even any butter!" Thoby's quip is pounced on by Clive as an opportunity to expound on the iniquities of English habit. We all laugh at the wit and agility of his sermon. While he is talking our soup arrives. I study its rich, dark color. I detect parsley, onion, fresh chives. I eat hungrily. When I look up I see that you have pushed your soup to one side. I sense your dislike of the unfamiliar food, your disgust at the stains on the tablecloth, the sudden, raucous bursts of laughter that erupt from the crowded tables. You are not enjoying yourself, your eyes signal, and you want me to share your discomfort. I look at Clive, at Thoby, at the rapid gesticulations of a man telling jokes at the bar, and decide to ignore you.

A woman enters the café, carrying roses. She nods to the owner and crosses to our table. She has seen we are foreigners and assumes, no doubt, we are easy prey. She sidles up to Clive. She has a shawl wound round her shoulders embroidered with exotic flowers and birds. She leans against Clive and lets her hand caress his cheek. He laughs at the liberty.

"Les roses. Mais bien sûr! Il faut des roses!" His pleasure in speaking French is obvious. He takes out his wallet and lays a handful of francs down on the table. The woman offers him her flowers.

"First, the ladies." Clive studies the roses for a moment, then dives in and pulls out two of the blooms. He presents me one with a flourish. I marvel at the flower's tightly whorled petals, its vivid red. You set the rose Clive offers you next to your glass, indifferent to the gesture. Clive selects a third bloom, trims the stem, and tucks it into Thoby's buttonhole. The woman scoops up the pile of coins and carries her bouquet to the neighboring table.

"That's what I love about the French! Their sense of enjoyment. Their love of flowers. It's what I admire about Manet. He'd paint that woman — in all her different angles. There'd be no posing, no falsification. We'd have her as she is — the rip in her dress, the sway of her hips as she moves between the tables, her keen commercial sense coupled with her unabashed joie de vivre!"

I am caught by Clive's enthusiasm. We order more wine. The waiter clears our dishes and sets plates of grilled fish in front of us, their skins glistening with lemon juice and oil. The smoke from our cigarettes unfurls in great vistas of unexplored terrain.

A nurse in a white uniform pushes open the door. You are standing by the window. As I go into the room you turn round. Your hair tumbles over your face and you look as if you have not changed your clothes for some time. There are stains on your blouse and a large tear in the hem of your skirt. I know better than to comment. I wait for the nurse to close the door on us. You stare at my shoes as I walk toward you. I put the parcels I have brought for you down on the narrow bed and begin to unwrap them.

"Here are the books you asked for in your letter, though Dr. Savage was quite firm when I spoke to him that you should only read for a very short time each day." I stack the books on the cabinet next to the bed. I sense you watching me. You move to the cabinet and pick up one of the books, hugging it to you like an old friend. It is Walter Raleigh's edition of Hakluyt.

"Savage would like to wrap me in cotton wool — or whatever the medicinal equivalent is. Does he not see that all this is *making* me ill?" Your hand gestures vaguely toward a shelf on which there are several half-empty glasses, each marked with a label.

"Veronal, chloral, paraldehyde. A sleeping draft to over-come the ill effects of the digitalis. Bromide to ward off the sleeping draft. A tincture for the headache brought on by the bromide. All this to be washed down by fifteen glasses of milk a day." You spin round and look at me.

"You know he wants to pull out my teeth."

I suddenly feel ashamed. I picture myself writing the letter to Dr. Savage, authorizing him to go ahead with his treatment. His description of the pockets of bacteria that gather in teeth and the impact these can have on the nervous system seemed entirely convincing. You open the Hakluyt.

"Thank you." Your voice is humble, a small child grateful for a favor. I can bear it no longer and hold out my hand.

We curl together on the bed. The walls of the nursing home vanish as we return to a time when we were little girls alone in the night nursery. You are my billy goat, my wombat, my mouse. I stroke your soft silky fur and feel you nuzzle my cheek. Your greedy ape lips are hungry and your teeth nibble playfully at my throat. I reach up and unfasten my dress and your baby mouth suckles my breast. I am your dolphin mother, glistening and sticky from your kisses. I will take you deep into the ocean where no one can harm us.

I walk through the deserted rooms, my notebook in my hand, and stop in front of each item of furniture, each painting, each silver-framed photograph and ornament. I must decide which of these items from our old life to carry with us and which to discard. I have the oddest sense, as I scrutinize each object and make my choice, that I am leaving the past behind. It is as if the process of appraisal peels away the layers of memory. I must disregard the image of Mother that floats into my mind as I consider her chair. The criteria I apply are practical and aesthetic. Is the chair useful or beautiful? If it is neither I resolve to sell it. I refuse to let my recollection of Mother sewing in her chair influence my judgment.

Bloomsbury has become so infamous! At the time, its main attractions were that it had a house we could afford and that it was not in the neighborhood of our aunts. As I look back now I see that moving there was a turning point. Yet I chose it almost by chance.

I cannot get used to the light that pours in through the windows of the new house. I kneel down on the bare floorboards and let it flood over me. I want to bask in it, purge myself in its rays, let its luminosity spur me.

Objects take on a new life in the plain, light rooms. The rich grains and delicate inlay of Mother's writing desk stand out for the first time. It is as if I am learning to see again. Colors radiate against the white walls, so that one of Mother's Indian shawls thrown over the back of a sofa, or a red rug unrolled on the hearth, suddenly fills a room. There are surprises. Leatherbound volumes from Father's library look sumptuous on the simple wooden shelves. I unpack Mother's photographs and after an hour of trying them in different places, decide to hang them in the hall. I see unexpected angles, unknown facets of her face. Even the past figures differently in the new space.

A wall of orange ablaze in the sun, the glow of hot coals. My colors have the sheen of silk, the rough textures of Hessian. In the top right-hand corner of my painting is a pale pink square, edged in blue. The clash between the pink and orange is violent, compelling, gorgeous. I mute it by adding a daub of white to the pink, but only slightly. I do not want to diminish the effect. On the left of my canvas I paint a series of rectangles. Some interconnect, some stand alone. I paint two of them blue — one a potent aquamarine, the other paler and tempered with the same hint of whiteness as the pink. I am careless with the outlines. I have had too many years of cloying detail. What interests me is the impact of the color. I want the immediate sensation, the unbroken panorama of shape and tone as you first enter a room.

In the center of my picture I paint a single rectangle. It is a rich, crimson red with traces of darker vermilion. It dazzles and sizzles against the orange. It is the corollary of Father and I revel in its daring. I turn my attention to the two remaining bars. I paint one green, a blue sage, slightly chalky. For the other I choose a strong burgundy.

I am fascinated by the way the different reds shun and call to each other. Sometimes, when I stand back from my canvas, I can see nothing else. The way the orange recedes against their impact astonishes me. I cannot believe the past has already lost its power. I turn my attention to my central rectangle. I am audacious. I will create the space I need. I will be mistress in my own house.

I did not forget you. I wrote to you every day. I implored you to eat well and rest, the doctors' litany. I made a study for you, found you a desk and chair, arranged your books. At the same time, I was grateful to Violet for taking you. I could not have coped with your convalescence on my own.

There was manipulation as well as helplessness in your loss of control. By relinquishing the burden to me, you ensured I remained in Mother's place, parenting you, indulging you, when we might both have renounced such roles. I was an easy accomplice. I might struggle against the call, I might even try to quell it, but my existence was not separate from yours.

I turn the kaleidoscope of memory, watch the shapes sift and fall. The truth is never easy. There was relief as well as terror in acknowledging your flaw. The gods had heaped too many gifts on you.

It amuses me now to think that what became so notorious, so much discussed, so revered in some quarters and satirized in others, began so humbly. Time has wrapped layers of myth and envy round what started very simply. A handful of young men and two nervous, ill-at-ease women seated round a fireplace. If you were writing this, you would know how to do the portrait of it, would add your own brilliant powers of observation, your vivacity and wit, your genius for describing the essence of a thing in a few consummate strokes. You would know how to render Saxon's exquisitely rolled umbrella, the lilt and halt of Lytton's queer pronunciation, Leonard's quavering hands. You would relish the long, awkward silences that so often preceded any debate, the clearing of a throat, eyes floorward, then a chance remark, beauty, perhaps, or truth, a word thrown into the air and bandied first this way, then that, until an entire, elaborate edifice of argument and counterargument had been constructed.

I thrilled to see the way your contribution wove itself in. I was as entertained as anyone by your originality. We were conspirators once again. I, welcoming and presiding; you, intellectually agile, eloquent, and daring. I took pleasure in watching the others lean forward, eager to catch you, inspired by what you said. I rejoiced in your triumphs. Your sport took place under my jurisdiction, for my entertainment. I was queen in my own house.

I have been blamed for my insularity, for my refusal to open my doors to a wider circle. I make no apologies. We had lived under the dominion of others for too long. There was a delicious freedom in being able to choose whom we associated with and on what terms.

I am old now. My fingers are twisted with arthritis. I look at my hand and try to remember it as it was, the skin smooth and unlined, the knuckles plump with flesh. Now, I would find it beautiful. Now I would recognize its sensuous aliveness. At the time I could not. To be told, so repeatedly and matter-of-factly, that one was attractive, as if it was a duty, as if it came with heavy penalties attached, stalled any burgeoning pride I might have had in my own potency. It is little wonder that we felt comfortable with Thoby's friends, the buggers, as you so roguishly called them. To them our appearance was neither an invitation nor a challenge. Taking their cue from Thoby they disregarded it, extending the permissive hand of friendship beyond the masks of our gender. Their approval ushered parts of us into being that had nothing to do with sex.

That is not entirely true. There was something else that came into play during those late-night discussions, a surfacing, a glimmering, like the first pink flush of sun spreading its beams over the horizon. I had seen the dawning before, when Stella married Jack. Now it was happening to me.

I am lying on the sofa with a length of silk draped over one arm. It is a remnant from a dress I have been making. The material is a startling cherry red and so beautiful I cannot bring myself to discard it. I try the silk round my shoulders, then wind it like a turban round my hair. You are sitting at the table by the window, writing. I can hear the rasp of your nib on the paper. I think of our conversation the previous evening. Lytton's voice trilled and faltered as he talked about love, and when I looked up from my sewing I found Clive staring at me intently. His eyes held mine for a moment, and I felt a sudden, dizzying exhilaration, like seeing a Tintoretto for the first time. I close my eyes to recapture the sensation, and when I open them again I am struck by my reflection in the mirror above the fireplace. With my head swathed in silk I look like an empress, majestic, supreme, reclining on her couch. I have one arm crooked behind my neck, and the angle amplifies the curve of my shoulders and breasts. I am voluptuous, a love goddess, carnal and bold.

You have seen it too. You have stopped writing, mesmerized. Our eyes catch, hover for an instant, before yours dip away. You return to your page, your brow furrowing with annoyance. You do not like this unfamiliar sister. I am slipping beyond your control. The red silk of my scarf slices us apart. I am as shocked as you are by my reflection in the mirror but I cannot tear my eyes away. I want to linger, consider this new persona, explore its untried possibilities. I listen to the furious scratch of your pen.

I paint on a wooden panel, large enough for a reclining nude. I curl the arms over the head, echoing its curve, then repeat the arch for the breasts and thighs drawn up close to the body. I lay my figure on wave-like daubs of blue. I want to give the impression that she is suspended, in water, perhaps, or air. I play with the colors. I mix gray and white to my pink, add traces of violet and gold. I want the flesh to look newly exposed, as if a sea creature has been peeled of its shell. I fill in the space above my figure quickly, great strikes of turquoise and ultramarine. I do not want to distract from her presence. I only want to close the space. I stand back and look at what I have done. The area above the figure is still too empty. I look at my colors. I decide to ignore verisimilitude altogether. My brush itches for red. I squeeze crimson onto my palette and blend it with my knife. This time, I paint spheres. I turn the arcs into poppies, vast wide-open blooms. Their black stamens are fresh rings against the red. There is still something missing. I have black left on my brush from the stamens and I draw a line between the poppies, lacing them together. I stand back and observe. Yes, the thread ties the whole. My picture is complete.

They come into the room, in groups of two or three. Henry arrives with Nina on his arm, followed by Beatrice and Ka. I spy Gwen talking to Marjorie in a corner, Mary and Silvia by the window. There is no formality. Today Clive has agreed to talk about emotion in art, but I am in no hurry for the proceedings to begin. I settle myself on a stool and look about me. Half my guests are in love with the innovations of the French, and half are appalled by them. I do not mind. What is important is that our focus is art. I think of Father's jeer that painting is a bastard sister to literature and wonder when you will make your entrance. You have already made it clear that you do not like my Friday gatherings. When I asked you at breakfast if you would hear Clive's talk your only response was to impress upon me the importance of the article you are engaged in writing. I wait until most of the guests have arrived, then signal to Clive. He takes his place in the chair by the fire and calls for quiet.

You appear as Clive begins to speak. I knew you could not keep away. You perch on a cushion by the door and I can tell you are caught by what Clive has to say. I see you lean forward, eager to hear more. Though you like to mock the painters, I sense that Clive's comments on composition intrigue you. When his talk is over you will return to your room and ponder all you have heard. You will apply his precepts to your writing. For all your affected disdain, it is my art that is showing you the way.

White linen suits with gray felt hats. White parasols lined in green. We stand on deck with Violet and watch the English cliffs recede into mist. This trip is the realization of a dream. For weeks now I have been poring over Greek architecture and sculpture, visiting the ancient Greece section in the British Museum. We are going back to the cradle of civilization. We are to travel alone to Patras, where we will join Thoby and Adrian. I stare into the channels the boat cuts through the glassy water and try to clear my mind. I have rejected Clive's proposal of marriage. Though I am certain it is the right decision, the words of his letter reel in my head, like the eddies that swirl against the boat or the sudden seasickness that comes over us as the coast disappears from view. It is not that I dislike Clive. On the contrary, his easy generosity, his ability to find pleasure in almost everything he encounters, have long been qualities I admire. I think of him sitting by the fireplace, his broad-ranging talk a balm compared to the straitjacket contributions of some of the others, and I remember the look in his eyes as he watched me sew. I shiver, though it is warm out on deck, and fasten my coat. I do not want marriage. I do not want to relinquish our newfound freedom. We are only just beginning our journey. I am not ready to turn back yet.

My thoughts undulate with the skyline. You wonder at my preoccupation. As we sail down the Adriatic, I paint the higgledy-piggledy clusters of houses I see clinging to the hill-sides on the mainland, the pinks and orange of bougainvillea and hibiscus.

I know even as we approach the port that something is wrong. A great weariness takes hold of me as we come into dock, so that even the few steps from the cabin to the gang-plank seem impossibly far. My limbs feel as if they have turned to water. My mind races, catching at snippets of conversation, fragments of memory, like a tuft buffeted by the wind. Images emerge from the seabed, drift for a moment, then vanish into the depths. Mother in her green dress flickers near the surface, then dissolves and reconfigures into your brooding jade eyes. I see Stella, Father. The forms that normally segregate people have become submerged in the seething waves.

When I look back to that time now, I ask myself what evil twist of fate it was that robbed me of my strength, of my power to in-tervene. If only I had not been so ill myself, perhaps I could have prevented what happened next from taking place. Or was my sickness a premonition, a resurgence of the terror that erupted with Mother's death and resurfaced again with Stel-la's? Was it a way of shielding myself from this new nightmare? As if by losing control the agony could not touch me.

Thoby. His smile was my smile as we mirrored each oth-er's expressions, his body my body as we chased each other under the nursery table or set off in pursuit of a toy. When he was diagnosed with typhoid I did not believe he could die. How could I admit that what was part of me was no more? It was inconceivable that he would not survive the operation the doctors ordered. I stared at his body laid out ready for burial, dry-eyed.

Once again it was your grief that allowed me to pass safely over the vortex, or so I thought at the time. I went on with my life while you wept. I wrote to Clive.

My body, languorous and feline, thrilling to his every move. Despite all that happened later, I will never forget the gift Clive made to me then. I cast around for images. Those that come immediately to mind, of fire or water or the sudden blossoming of fruit trees in the spring, are tired and imprecise. It was as if his gentle, practiced fingers slowly stroked away a layer of dull varnish, releasing the hues and textures of the paint so that the figure could come alive at last. I did not know it was possible to experience such pleasure in one's body. We spent long afternoons learning the secrets of each other's delight. We netted life in the warmth of our embraces and together banished all thoughts of death. For the moment we were inviolable.

The clip clop of the horses' hooves as I drive in the carriage George has borrowed for my wedding day signals the start of a new era. I smooth the satin folds of my dress and wonder at what I am about to do. I think of Mother's admonitions, her insistence that marriage is the goal of a woman's life. I am fulfilling her prophecy. I feel a glow of satisfaction as I reflect that I have done it all on my own. The man I am about to marry is of my choosing.

I am so happy I hardly take in the ceremony. There is a hail of confetti as we come out of the church. Clive takes my arm and steers me through the groups of well-wishers. I gaze at the streets on the way to the station through a veil of hope.

We are too late for the train. Clive paces up and down on the platform, smoking. I take refuge in the waiting room. I settle myself on the hard wooden bench and look about me. I watch the hands of the clock on the wall opposite. I am eager to embark. I can hear Clive talking to the stationmaster. A man walks past the window and raises his hat, a tribute to my bridal dress. I feel vulnerable and suddenly afraid. I pick up my bag and take out my notebook and pen. The writing restores me. I am calm again. The loops of my letters spin the thread that connects me to you.

"Darling Billy."

4

THERE IS A KNOCK ON THE DOOR. CLIVE PULLS THE
sheet over our heads and puts his finger to his lips. I bite my
cheek to stop myself from giggling. Clive curls a loop of my
hair round his finger.

The door opens. We hear the tread of footsteps on the floorboards.

"In flagrante delicto!" It is Lytton. Clive groans.

"Confound it, can one not have an hour's peace with one's
wife?"

"Ha! So you call upon the sanctity of marriage, do you? I,
by contrast, prefer the honesty of feeling . . . Tell me, is there
no chair in your boudoir that is not entirely filled with your
clothes?"

Clive throws back the sheet and we see Lytton, displaying a
pair of my knickers from the end of his cane. He bows to us,
waving the garment like a flag.

"Sir. Madam. I trust your pleasure was replete."

I lean my head on Clive's shoulder and listen to the men tossing jokes backward and forward between then. My daring astounds me. I run my hand across Clive's naked chest and think of the rigid codes of conduct that governed the past. My mind flits from Mother's attempts to teach us self-denial to the endless afternoons of tea-table talk, where it was impossible to say what one thought. I have spent my life obeying other people's orders and am only now breaking free. Under the sheet, I caress the responding hardness of Clive's sex with unashamed abandon. Here, I can say and do what I like. I plot mauve and yellow curtains for our sitting room, determine to spurn Aunt Mary's invitation. The edifices of convention have been razed to the ground. I will take my art to its limits.

The figures bend in the same direction, the ovals of their heads incline together. I work the circumference of his shoulder, the hoop of his tailcoat as it fans out behind. I create his apparel with streaks of color — purple, brown, black, palest pearly green. My dancer must not be static. Fluidity is his essence. I wrap the woman's body around his, repeating the curve for her flank and thigh. Her arm reaches across his in an exaggerated bow. She leans on him, eyes closed, while he contains and directs her. I mix mustard yellow and ocher for her dress, applying it in thick bands. She is the beloved, after all. She must have the primary place. I worry that my figures lack solidity. I use black to enhance their outlines, to define the features of their faces. I accentuate the folds of his jacket, the dark pleats of her dress as it falls across her breast. The grid I have drawn to block out the space is still visible. I decide to keep it in. It sets my figures in a world apart. I like it that the mechanics of my invention are still present. The background must be decorative, gay. I choose earth colors — terra cotta, sienna, burnt umber. I concoct a frame round my couple, more ovals. My lattice is both open and enfolding. The dancers are vulnerable. They must be protected from the demons of this world.

I unwrap the glasses from their tissue paper and place them on a tray. Clive found the glasses in Paris and we carried them home in our luggage. They are old and each one is slightly different. When I have finished I put the tissue paper back in the box and look about me. I hardly recognize the room. It is full of the things Clive has brought. There are new carpets and cabinets and chairs. Mauve curtains hang in the windows, their yellow linings vibrant in the light. Everything feels modern, opulent, alive.

My portrait of Nelly Cecil is on the mantelpiece. There are some crudenesses in the execution but I am pleased with the result. I have painted Nelly reading by a window. Her eyes, the dark mass of her hair, are accentuated by the black of her dress and the somber colors of the drape behind. I plan to exhibit the portrait. I have already shown it to Margery, who thinks it the best thing I have done.

You arrive early. You stand in the doorway, noticing the changes. Clive kisses you on both cheeks. You bristle.

"We are enjoying the story you sent us." My peace offering works. Clive winks at me above your head as he picks up the relay.

"Yes. I particularly liked the explanatory passages, where the prose was less wrought. It had an immediate quality I felt some of the more poetic writing lacked."

You perk up at Clive's praise. You can never resist an opportunity to talk about your work.

"I often wonder if I shouldn't go with my first thoughts on things. They usually come out more directly. The trouble begins when I read what I've written and realize all the nuances that aren't yet planted in my words."

Clive is watching you. I see you smile at him. It is a smile I know.

"Ginny, I need your help with the food. The others will be here soon." Clive is mine and I will not let you steal him. I shepherd you into the dining room, where the table is set for a buffet lunch. I pass you a basket of cutlery which must be sorted and wrapped into napkins.

We work alongside each other without speaking. I finish my share of the cutlery and take the fruit out of its bag. I sense you studying me. I arrange oranges and apples on a plate, sculpting them into a tempting mound. I glance at your hands as you fold the linen squares and notice how pale they are. I want to ask how you are feeling but do not dare. I break a grape from its stem and offer it to you. You shake your head and I pop the fruit into my own mouth. Its juice is bittersweet on my tongue.

Several of the guests have arrived when we return to the drawing room. Gwen congratulates me on my picture and I accompany her to the fireplace. Clive puts a record on the gramophone, another of his gifts. Nina pulls Henry up to dance. I feel Clive's arm encircle my waist. His hands are warm on my bare skin. As Clive steers me across the floor the soft folds of my skirt swirl round me like a fan. Light pours through the windows and I am conscious of everyone looking at me. The music finishes and I whisper in Clive's ear. He nods and makes his way toward you. I watch him loop his arm round your shoulder as Ka sets the music going again. For a few steps you follow Clive, your movements an awkward imitation of his. Leonard comes to talk to me, and when I search for you again Clive is dancing with Mary. You are nowhere to be seen.

I catch up with you in the hall. You have your coat on and are fastening the buttons.

"You're not leaving." I stand in front of you. You glare at me angrily.

"You set him up to do that. You want to make me look ridiculous."

I shrug. "I thought you'd like someone to dance with."

"I don't want your pity! You're so unfair! You have everything — Clive, money, people wanting your pictures — whereas I have nothing . . ." Your voice trails away. You gesture vaguely toward the drawing room. "You must see how we all worship you."

I stare at the floor. I do not know what to say.

"Ness . . . I was thinking about Mother the other night. Do you remember, when she died, how terrified we were when the undertakers came to take away her body?"

I gulp. I see the two of us clinging to each other on the landing as the men carry Mother's coffin down the stairs. I rally. I must not let you drag me back to the past. Through the open door I hear snatches of music.

"You'll find someone. You could marry tomorrow if only you would let yourself."

I catch your surprise and drive my point home.

"Walter is clearly smitten. He can hardly take his eyes off you. And Lytton tells anyone who will listen that you are the most brilliant woman he knows."

You are gazing at me now, your face flushed.

"You're beautiful, Billy. Men are interested in you. All they need is for you to encourage them a little."

I hold out my arm. You slip your coat from your shoulders and link yours through mine. I lead you back to the party.

What law is it that says one will be confronted by the very thing one loathes? You always teased me for my tendency to exaggerate, but even I cannot do justice to the awfulness of Cleeve House. There were many problems in growing up as we did but there were also compensations. We were surrounded by examples of achievement born from endeavor. The benefits of hard work were inculcated in us from an early age. Clive's family home could not have been more different. How shall I describe its deadly blend of leisure without purpose, lavishness without taste? The snobbery and prejudices of Clive's parents and sisters turned every encounter into a trying ordeal. The extended visits Clive insisted on were the first hurdles I had to navigate in our marriage. I was accustomed to painting for several hours each day and felt frustrated when I could not. I grew restless. I began to dream of escape.

How I miss you! I sit in the dressing room I have converted into a makeshift studio and stare at my palette. Through the open window I can hear Clive's sister organizing the riders, her voice a peremptory bark. I go over and close the window. I cannot bear to hear any more. I have argued with Clive and the thought makes me wretched. I tried to explain my need to paint regularly but Clive's only response was to tease. He told me that in his view if things did not come easily it was probably a signal to stop. I am beginning to despise his halfhearted attitude to working. I fear that for all his brilliance Clive will never produce anything of note. I think of the long hours Father spent laboring in his study, Mother's commitment to nursing despite all the demands on her time. Their motto was sacrifice and dedication, words I sense are anathema to Clive.

It all started as we were alone in our dressing room after breakfast. I tried to persuade Clive not to accompany the others but to stay with me and write. For twenty minutes we worked in companionable silence. Then Clive pushed his books to one side.

"This is absurd. I feel about as fertile as an old newspaper."

I look up.

"You need to give it time. Just sit with it a little and something will emerge."

For a while Clive accepts my advice and we are quiet again. I return to mixing my paints. Finally Clive loses patience.

"Oh come on, Nessa! It's a glorious day. Far too lovely to be stuck in here. Let's ride with the others and then stop somewhere and have lunch. What do you say?"

I gaze at the floor. We rode yesterday, and the day before. If I give in to Clive there will be no further chance to paint today. I think of all the hours you and I spent working together in the conservatory at home. As I broke off and looked at what I had done, the sound of your pen crossing your page was all the incentive I needed to continue. I sigh.

"You go. I'd like to stay. There will be plenty of people on the ride. No one will miss me."

I finish preparing my palette. As I clean my brushes I look out the window and see Clive arm in arm with a striking dark-haired woman. I wonder who she is.

I try to settle back to work. Your last letter is on the chair beside me and I pick it up. Here, I am a beached dolphin, lashing about for water on the sand. I need your words to re-vive me.

Your description of a breakfast argument with Adrian makes me want to laugh out loud! You conjure the scene for me, the sticky yellow dribbles as you pelt an egg and it explodes against the wall. I put your letter in my pocket and imagine you writing, a slight furrow in your brow as you lean over your page. I pick up my pencil and draw your face. I mark the almonds of your brows, the fine chiseling of your nose. I find pastels and shade the pearly rose of your skin, the green glints in your eyes. I add color to your lips, accentuate the bow I should so much like to kiss. I cannot wait until I see you again.

You come at last. I race to greet you. All day I have longed for you to arrive. Clive has arranged supper for us in the parlor so that we can escape the interrogations of his family. I loop my arm through yours as I escort you. You are wearing a dress I do not recognize, sea green and cut low at the neck. As we enter the parlor you seat yourself in one of the armchairs. Clive pours you a glass of wine.

"Here. You'll need this after your journey."

You take the wine and smile at Clive.

"Thank you. Actually I hardly noticed the journey. I had a new idea for that piece I sent you. You were right that the prose was too feverish. I spent the whole time rewriting it."

I tell myself I should not be surprised if you want to talk to Clive about your work. For some time now the two of you have been corresponding about your novel. I know he encourages you. I rein in my desire to have you to myself and resolve not to interrupt.

"I'm glad my comments were helpful." Clive pours two more glasses of wine and, after handing one to me, perches in the chair beside you.

"I've been trying to get back to the dream-like quality I had when I started it. I want to show that the men and women are different but I don't want to preach. I quite agree that like God one shouldn't. The effect I want is one of running water. Everything fluid and broad and deep."

You look beautiful as you speak. You are leaning forward, your eyes lit with your vision. Your free hand gesticulates as if it is miming the water. I see that Clive is transfixed.

"There is no doubt your writing has a magical quality to it. Sometimes when I read you it's as if I'm holding a live bird in my hand. I feel its heart beating, then look on in rapture as it opens up its wings and takes to the sky. There are very, very few writers who can do that."

I have a sudden, painful image of you as a successful writer, sought after and feted while my own pictures go unnoticed. I feel excluded and second-rate. Despite the promise I have made to myself I burst out.

"Clive and I have been wondering how your harem is faring!" I turn and face you. "Have you spoken to Sydney since you refused him?"

Clive laughs. "Poor Waterlow! I can't say I am surprised, though. Now, what kind of creature will you have, I wonder . . ."

"Ah! There's the rub." I know from your tone that I have played straight into your hands. The topic of your suitors has piqued Clive's interest. For the first time since your arrival you toss me a gleeful smile.

"First loves are difficult to replace — as all dolphins know."

I look away. Such public declarations embarrass me. You turn back to Clive.

"As to who I should like to make my life's companion — I do not honestly know that such a being exists."

Grace has put a vase of flowers on my desk, red and yellow chrysanthemums and papery autumn leaves. I look out the window at the garden. In a few weeks the leaves will be down. Already there are great piles swirling about the lawn. I crinkle one of the leaves in the vase and watch it flake into confetti in my fingers. I did not tell Clive I was pregnant that first autumn. I kept the slow swell of my belly, the dawning realization that I was carrying a new life, to myself. When I finally broke the news to Clive I watched his face alter from pride through fear to regret. As I grew bigger his attitude to me became more distant. We no longer spent lascivious afternoons exploring each other's pleasure. Wounded by his rejection I turned in on myself, focusing my energies on the coming baby.

If you had had children, you would have been able to describe what it has always seemed to me impossible to express. You would have known how to carry language into the mute hinterland of the body, where what happens is governed by an invisible force. I had not expected the unremitting pain of labor, the violent dips and peaks of terror and hope. I can still remember the awe of holding my newborn infant. A pact was established between us as I prized open his tiny fingers and felt them curl tight again round mine. The gesture sealed a pledge to love and protect this child always. It was a promise neither you nor Clive understood.

∽

I watch your heads disappear past banks of peonies and sweet William, tall columns of hollyhocks and delphiniums. My baby is asleep in his crib, quiet at last. I should have liked to stride out with you along the cliff path and feel the stiff breeze blowing off the sea. I should have liked to stop and gaze at the basin of undulating blue. Now I might have turned my attention to your conversation. I could have joined in your discussion of Lytton's book. I know my fretting over the baby annoys you. I know you wish I could leave him to settle by himself. I see your look of jealous disapproval every time I pick him up. There have been many disappointments since the birth. I have borne Clive's panic as I have tried to give the baby to him, braved his irritation whenever the baby cries. I have watched Clive move steadily away from me. He no longer sleeps in my bed. You have become his ally. You vindicate his feelings, commiserate with him and spur him on.

Yesterday, as we were alone together, you accused me of forgetting you, my firstborn. Where were your kisses, your pettings? you demanded angrily, as I took the baby onto my lap. You insisted I had turned my back on you, had invited you to Cornwall without really wanting you there. You complained I had no right to call the baby Julian, Thoby's first name. I was unkind and selfish and ridiculous to boot. Thoby was not mine to resurrect. You would get your revenge, you shouted as you left the room to look for Clive, I should not have things all my own way.

Was that it? The eye of the past winks at me, a reminder that its mysteries remain unsolved. I see now that Clive was a willing accomplice in your work of destruction. You accompanied him on his walks, beguiled him with your stories, seduced

him with your coruscating prose. Strengthened by his guid-
ance, your writing emerged as a powerful force. People started
to hear of you. In some part of myself, I needed your triumph.
I cradled my baby and took perverse comfort in knowing you
were a success. Preoccupied with Julian, I had little energy
for painting. While my ambitions lay dormant, I hoped your
achievements might stand for us both.

You look extraordinary. Disguised as Cleopatra, you are wearing a golden headdress, a tight beaded bodice, and a long
straight skirt. Your eyes and lips are so vividly made up that
at first I do not recognize you. You have wound a bracelet on
your bare left arm to look like a snake. People crowd round
you.

I stand beside one of the ornamental trees and wonder if I
should make my way across to you. I only came to the party
at Clive's insistence. I have no costume and feel out of place
amongst the gaudily dressed guests. My clothes do not fit and
my hair has lost its luster since the birth. Before I can decide,
a woman I do not know comes toward me. She holds out her
hand like an old friend. When she speaks it is with an Ameri-
can accent.

"It *is* you! I was just saying to Cecil here how I was sure it
was you. I've seen your photograph. You are every bit as lovely
as I imagined."

I blush despite myself. It is a long time since anyone has
paid me a compliment.

"Now — may we pry? — do tell us what delicious thing you
are engrossed in preparing. I said to myself as soon as I saw you
standing here all alone, Lydia, do not be fooled, that woman
is busy observing us for her next great work. Who knows? Per-

haps I shall figure in it. Though that really would be presumptuous of me."

I draw back from the woman's coquettish smile. I do not understand. Does she mean I might paint her? She detects my confusion and laughs.

"Oh, don't mind me! I love to tease. I was just wondering — you see I should so much like the opportunity to talk to you — if I might ask you about Henry James. I thought your review of *The Golden Bowl* quite wonderful. Do you really think him one of the greatest living novelists? After all, you British have so many distinguished writers of your own. Such a compliment to pay us Americans!"

"I'm sorry. It's my sister — Virginia — who writes. My name is Vanessa. I'm a painter."

The woman stares at me in disbelief for a moment, then mutters something incoherent and hurries away. I gaze after her, glad that the tree is there to screen me. Finally I pluck up courage and make my way over to you.

"So you've come to say hello at last." I study the thick gold and black bands you have painted round each of your eyes. You look like a courtesan. You are arm in arm with a tall, copper-haired woman in a black Spanish mantilla I recognize as Ottoline Morrell. Your intimacy surprises me. The only time I have heard you talk about the famous society hostess was to ridicule her. You point at me with ring-covered fingers.

"It's so refreshing to see you without your appendage. I had started to think of your body as permanently misshapen — inseparable from the large, mewling infant you had attached to your hip."

I ignore you and shake hands with Ottoline. You refuse to be flouted.

"As a matter of fact, Ottoline and I were just talking about babies. I was telling her mine will be entirely made of paper. Paper and words, of course."

I realize from the slur in your speech how drunk you are.

"Ottoline has experience with both kinds of progeny. We've been setting out the merits and faults in each case. The labor is roughly the same — though there is perhaps more blood in the case of written offspring — but this is amply compensated for by other advantages. After all, books do not grow up and turn their backs on their aging creators."

There is a flare of triumph in your eyes. I look round for Clive. You seem to read my mind.

"Now where's that delicious husband of yours? I sent him to fetch ices. Cleopatra must have her Antony. Ah, there he is, returning from his arduous campaign. He appears to be victorious."

You beckon to Clive, who is holding a tray of ices above his head as he battles his way through the throng of guests. I wave to him but he does not see me. I watch his eyes fasten on you.

"Here we are." Clive hands you an ice, then offers one to Ottoline. To my surprise, you link your arm through mine. I follow you reluctantly across the courtyard. We stop by the fountain.

"I'm glad you're here. Ott can be so ridiculous! She worships all artists but can never quite decide to set her coronet aside, so everything she says is tinged with an overbearing condescension. Look at her flirting with Clive! She's like some terrifying Medusa with her great beaky face."

I stare at you. I do not know whether I am shocked at the way you tear Ottoline to pieces or relieved that you are once again confiding in me.

❧

I soothe myself with color. I squeeze rivulets of orange, blue, mauve onto my palette and brush them straight onto the paper. I am not painting. I only wish to console myself. I let the sweep of the blue across the white blank out my fury. All morning I have sat by the window and watched for the pair of you to come back from your walk. I have calmed Julian's feverish crying and imagined the two of you alone together on the sand. I have not slept well. The room is hot and stuffy and I long for the bracing sea air. I refill my brush with mauve and continue my wash of color. Julian frets in his cot and I rock him for a moment until he settles. Suddenly I crave black. I picture your hand resting lightly on Clive's arm, your eyes glancing up at him as you ask him a question. I know your naivety arouses Clive's desire and that he will try to kiss you. I work bars of black that tear my colors to shreds. Orange is rent asunder, blue and mauve are prized apart.

Did some of this touch you? Did some of my murderous, self-preserving anger reach you as you walked along the shore that day? Was there a moment when you looked up and saw a shark's fin lance the water, or the dip of a bird's wing pierce the unending blue? Was it at this point, as you let Clive guide you over the shingle, that doubts began to fissure your mind, made you tremble and draw back?

A porcelain jar in the shape of an urn, mounted on a small plinth. No one can deny its beauty, its cool serenity, its almost regal presence. The decoration is very precise, a crown of leaves at the base, a frieze of blue flowers round the rim. There is something inviolable about the jar, as if it must retain its secret to the end. Next to it I place two smaller objects. On the right, there is a stoppered bottle, labeled like the medicine vials Father kept by his bed. I paint it green, virile, tightly corked. On the left I work an open dish, empty for the moment of contents. It has a look of expectancy about it, as if it already knows its fate. I turn my attention to the background. Here I need light, shadow, space. I want to suggest there is hope in the blankness. In front of the objects I fashion poppies, another group of three. I work delicately, painstakingly. The two that are furthest from the viewer I make white, their petals closed, merging into the shadow. The third I paint red, the color spilling from the petals like blood. I do not see any meaning in my flowers. I refuse to say which of them is me or Clive or you. I create the stems long and slender, lying across the canvas in parallel. I do not allow them to touch.

5

I RECOGNIZE HIM IMMEDIATELY. I HANG BACK, SHIELD-
ing myself behind Clive, uncertain if he will remember me.
He is at the far end of the platform, studying the train time-
table. He looks up suddenly, as if conscious of my gaze, and
his eyes light with recognition. The next moment he is hurrying toward us.

We share a carriage. I observe the deep lines in Roger's face,
his shock of white hair, the surprising contrast of his ink-black
brows. While he chats with Clive I look out the window and
let my thoughts drift. I remember Desmond and Molly's party
and how alarmed I was when I discovered I had been seated
next to Roger Fry. His reputation as an artist and critic, his en-
cyclopedic knowledge, his searching questions as he quizzed
me on my work made me tongue-tied at first. Yet as the evening progressed my feelings toward him changed. He encouraged me to speak, persuaded me that my opinions mattered.
His enthusiasm led me to formulate thoughts I did not know I
had. I grew increasingly bold as our conversation ranged from

Sargent to the French, the wonders of the Italian Renaissance to the blunders of English design. By the end of the dinner I felt I had known Roger all my life. At the same time, it was his unfamiliarity, the daring in not quite knowing how he would react, that made the encounter exciting.

I listen to Clive and Roger discuss travel, mutual acquaintances, art. I make no attempt to join in. I focus on the bright planes of light created by the speeding train, the mercurial green of the passing fields. I do not fail to notice Roger's kindness. Nor the way he looks at me whenever there is a lull in his talk with Clive.

The next time I see Roger is in London. He dines with us at Gordon Square. It is one of my first parties since Quentin's birth and I am anxious that it should go well. As we leave the table for the drawing room Roger catches up with me. We stand facing each other in the chilly hallway. It is Roger who speaks first.

"How is your new baby?"

The gentleness in his voice hits home. Suddenly I cannot stop myself from crying. Tears slide down my cheeks, splash onto my dress, splatter onto the floor. All my pent-up feelings, all the anxiety and exhaustion and bitterness I have carried inside me ever since Quentin was born, well up and overwhelm me. Prompted by the concern of this almost stranger I pour out torment after torment. I tell Roger about Clive's indifference to his two sons and how I am too tired to paint. I tell him my new baby will not gain weight and that I think you are having an affair with Clive. Roger catches each of my torments and holds them fast. He weighs them in his hands. Then he leads me back into the deserted dining room and casts about for solutions.

❧

Mother's necklace is as beautiful as I remember. My hand trembles as I take it out of its box and hold it against my throat. The gems catch the light as I look in the mirror. It is the first time I have worn it since she died.

Clive comes toward me struggling with his tie.

"Damned thing! I can't seem to get it right. Sometimes it knots beautifully, without any apparent effort, and at other times it's the devil's own job to make a decent bow."

I hook the clasp on Mother's necklace and turn round.

"Here. Let me try."

Clive stoops so that I can reach the tie from my stool. As I lift my arms to fasten it he kisses me fondly. I rest my head against his chest for a moment and smell his familiar scent of soap and eau de cologne. Then I knot his tie. Clive bends to examine the result in the mirror.

"I'd forgotten how adept you are."

His hands caress my shoulders and his fingers stray to Mother's necklace.

"It suits you. I hope your dinner partner appreciates how lovely you look."

I blush, grateful for the compliment. Despite all the talks we have had about the need for self-fulfillment and the hypocrisy of convention, I am still not used to our separate arrangements. I ask the question I dread.

"Will the goat be at the party?" At the mention of your nickname, Clive pulls away. In the mirror I see him frown.

"She is certainly invited. That doesn't mean she will come, of course. She's quite the celebrity these days. Everybody wants to know her."

I watch Clive concentrate on his cuff links. I am not fooled by his apparent indifference. I decide to delve a little deeper.

"Did I tell you she was certain Quentin would be a girl? I said I'd call her Clarissa if she were. She seemed to like that."

I bite my tongue. I have dared to mention you and the baby in the same breath. To my surprise, Clive grins.

"She showed me a story she had written a few weeks ago that had a woman called Clarissa in it. I would be careful if I were you."

Clive loops a twist of my hair that has fallen loose back into place. I reach up and touch his hand. He gives me a reassuring pat.

"Well, see you tomorrow."

As I watch the door close behind him I am seized with a sudden panic. I know that even if I call him back he will not come. I remind myself that I must not stifle him, that if I want to keep him I must allow him to be free. I stare at myself in the mirror. Mother's necklace shimmers and sparkles in the glass. I unhook it and lay it carefully in its box. I wind a silk scarf round my throat. Then I go downstairs to meet Roger.

Constantinople, like a dish of soap bubbles, ethereal against the sky. One morning Roger and I escape together for a painting expedition to the hills, leaving Clive and Harry to continue their tour of historic monuments alone. We set our easels in an olive grove, delighting in the silver-green leaves and darker jade of the unripe fruit, the rusts and ochers of the parched earth. An old man appears on a donkey and dismounts to watch us work. Roger, ebullient as ever, engages him in a conversation that consists mainly of gestures and a handful of frequently repeated words. When we have finished painting, the old man beckons us to follow him. He indicates that he wishes to offer us something to drink. We pack our things and accompany him to a low stone house. The man disappears inside and returns almost immediately with his wife. He mimes that he would like us to sketch her. We oblige, glad for this opportunity to rest. It is cool inside the house after the searing sunshine. I take out my sketchbook and begin to draw the woman. The old man brings a pot of coffee and four small, decorated glasses. He serves the coffee black with several spoonfuls of sugar. It is so sweet I can hardly drink it. I finish my portrait and show it to the woman. She claps her hands in rapture, thrilled with the likeness I have caught. Then she takes me outside to the well so that I can wash. The water is deliciously cold and I let it splash over my fingers. I dip the edge of my scarf in the water and wipe it over my face and neck. It is only as I am drying my hands that I notice my ring is gone. I stare at the slight red mark round my finger where the ring should be and realize it must have slipped off in the icy water. My consternation brings the men outside. The old man fetches a mirror and we peer into the well, hoping to see the jewels flash in the reflected light. After several minutes of fruitless searching the woman bursts into tears. I am forced to comfort her, pretend that it does not matter. Roger tries to cheer me with descriptions of all the wonderful rings he has seen for sale in the local bazaar. He promises to buy me another. I dare not confess that the ring I have lost was Clive's engagement ring.

I lie under the open window of our hotel, catching the sounds that drift in from outside, and mourn my dead baby. I hear children playing in the courtyard below and remember the sluice of blood that streamed between my legs. I listen to the women's voices as they scrub the floors, the footsteps of other guests as they pass the door to my room. The sounds come at me through a gauze, as if I am disconnected from the world. I stare at the ceiling, trying to decipher the thread of a memory in the veins and cracks of the ceiling. I watch the water splash over my fingers and my ring slip into the well. I feel my hand in Clive's and the imprint of my fingers on Roger's skin. I recall the passion of Roger's kiss and the excruciating guilt as my stomach cramps in pain. I see the shape of an infant in the clots of blood. Always it is as if the memory takes place just ahead of me, so that I am powerless to intervene. Then the images fizz and blur until all the elements twist together and Roger and Clive and I are part of some hideous beast. I tremble and scream and call out to the beast to beware, warning it of the murder it is about to commit. Sometimes I lash out and try to separate the bodies. Sometimes I lie motionless, sobbing to find the pictures of my life becoming so vengeful.

Water. Perhaps because of the oppressive heat of the Turkish summer I think constantly of water. I feel as if I am on a precipice and that at any moment I might fall into an abyss from which I shall not return. I watch myself plunge headlong, both dreading and longing for the fall. I can no longer contain the mechanisms of my body, the wild ravings of my mind. Only water can obliterate what I have done. Only drowning will thwart the monsters I might still create.

It is Roger who brings me back from the precipice. It is his hand that soothes away my terrors, his voice that coaxes me back to life. Day after day, night after night, he sits with me, reassuring me that I am not going mad. I cling to his hand, his voice, his faith in me. They are the beacons guiding me to safety.

Unskilled, vulgar, offensive! I can see the headlines still. The furor Roger's exhibition of French painting caused is something it is now difficult to imagine. To understand it, one has to go back to Edwardian England, with its hankering after convention, its abhorrence of change. To a society that buried dissent beneath the plush carpets of its ruling elite, the aggressive exuberance of a Manet or Gauguin was shocking in the extreme. The French painters opened the floodgates for experiment and individual expression. The hallowed mimesis of English art was shaken to its core.

A high-ceilinged room with white walls. The dazzle of the paintings is so fierce I am forced to lower my eyes. I am still shaky from my weeks of illness and at first I am unable to take in the cacophony of colors and shapes. When I do raise my eyes I am momentarily blinded by crimson and yellow and swathes of blue. I catch my breath. I have scarcely ever seen anything so exciting. I feel a flutter of elation in my breast, as if the pictures have touched a chord that has not been sounded until now.

Roger takes hold of my arm and leads me to a landscape by Cézanne. I see from a glance that its colors are quieter than those of the other canvases, but even so I cannot look at it in its entirety. Instead, I study a small patch of sienna toward the bottom right-hand corner, picked out in white, black, gray. It might be a huddle of cottages. I note the deliberateness of the brush strokes, the way color is laid over color so that while cottages are hinted at it is the overall effect that is important. I can tell from the pressure of Roger's hand on my arm that he is as spellbound as I am. Slowly, he raises his free hand and points to a bank of green. The swirls and daubs suggest foliage, but what is even more extraordinary is the way the cluster creates an impression of distance while remaining part of the larger pattern. I move a step backward. I look at the whole painting now. I let myself take in the blues and whites of the mountain-top, my eye dropping back down the canvas to trace their echo through browns and greens. A streak of purple at the base of the picture makes me want to laugh for pure joy. It has no jus-tification for being there apart from its echoing of the moun-tain motif. Roger catches my mood. He points to a woman in a lilac dress backing away from a Matisse nude, shocked by its crude depiction of fuchsia flesh. As the woman turns, her skirt flares out behind her, and without realizing it she becomes part of the exhibition, mirroring the line of purple in the Cé-zanne. I return to his landscape. This time my eye is caught by a horizontal bar that runs from the right-hand side toward the center. Is it a road, or a bridge? I see that it does not mat-ter. Without it, the painting would be a chaos of forms. It is the pivotal line on which the rest hangs.

I cannot look anymore. I turn to Roger. He understands at once and guides me through the crowd of people to a quiet room off the main gallery. He holds me in his arms and I press my face into his jacket. He knows without my saying anything how much the exhibition has meant to me.

"Perhaps Clive will buy the Cézanne," I say at last, reluctant to relinquish its hold.

Roger lifts my face and kisses it.

"Perhaps you will paint your own masterpieces."

I am glad we have arranged to go in together. As we make our way to the cloakroom I feel unexpectedly shy. The out-fits seemed perfect as I leafed through the catalog in the cos-tumier's, searching amongst flouncy ball gowns and routine pantomime wear for something appropriate, but now that we are here I am less certain. For Roger's party, I wanted an outfit that would match the vitality of his exhibition, and when I saw the sketch of a grass skirt with paper-flower garlands I thought I had found it.

"How about if we go dressed as South Sea Islanders?" I asked as you hovered in the doorway. "We could be Gauguin's women." You hid beneath the brim of your hat. I sensed your dislike of the mirrors, the tailors' dummies, the inquisitive stares of the shop girls wondering which costumes we would choose. Perhaps it was your disquiet that made me bold. I ordered the outfits.

Fortunately, the cloakroom is deserted. We are late and most of the guests have already arrived. I have spent the afternoon with Roger, showing him my new designs. He will take them for his workshop and I still feel elated by his praise. I undo my coat and remove my shoes and stockings. If we are to do this properly we must be barefoot. I have brought the garlands in a bag and I stand in front of the mirror to arrange them.

"What do you think?" I slide a flower behind my ear and turn round.

"You look . . . glorious!" You stare at my naked breasts, only partly hidden by the paper flowers. I have a sudden, fleeting memory of dressing for one of George's soirees, and think how far I have traveled since then. I am no longer constrained by outmoded rules, no longer in thrall to the old masters. What propels me now is passion.

"Come on."

You let your coat fall to the floor. We grin at each other in our outlandish garb. I untie your hair and let it fall loose across your shoulders. I wind flower garlands round your torso. When I have finished you put your hands on my waist and we dance a few paces, gyrating our hips so that our grass skirts rustle.

Soon we are giggling like schoolgirls. We loop arms and enter the fray.

Several heads turn our way as we push through the throngs of guests. I see Roger in the distance talking to a group of people but decide not to join him. Instead, I steer you toward a quiet corner.

"So, is it true? Clive says Gerald is to publish your novel."

"Yes." Your eyes light with pleasure. I cannot help thinking how easy it has been for you as a writer, with so much family support.

"And will I like it?"

"I hope so . . . You know most of what I do is for you." There is a faint note of pleading in your voice. You pause. "I'm afraid I'm a long way behind the painters, though, in understanding design."

Your frankness touches me. I want to return the confidence.

"We've both had so much to unlearn."

"I think you've gone further than I have. There is no doubt painting is leading the way. Fiction has forgotten its purpose. The novelists circle round their subject, describing everything that is extraneous to it, and then are surprised when it slips from view."

Before I can reply, I become aware of Roger waving at me from the other side of the room. You see him too.

"There's Roger. Shall we go over?"

I hesitate. I wonder if you have guessed that Roger and I are lovers. I have a sudden desire to keep this relationship to myself.

"No. I thought I saw Lytton just now. He wrote to me the other day and said that Leonard Woolf was on his way home from Ceylon. Let's go and talk to him. I'd like to find out more about Leonard. By all accounts he has made a great success of his time out there."

I pull you to your feet and let my voice drop to a whisper.

"Lytton also told me Leonard is looking for an English wife."

I wink at you.

"He could be just the thing."

I have been expecting it for days. I rip open the brown paper packaging and feel its weight in my hands. Your first novel. I cannot bring myself to read it straightaway. Instead, I open it at random and skim a few sentences. The crispness of the prose does not surprise me, to that I am accustomed. What astonishes me is your audacity.

"We are suffering the tortures of the damned," said Helen.

"This is my idea of hell," said Rachel.

Somewhere in my head a warning bell rings. Your words transport me back to the dances we were forced to attend with George. I see us whispering conspiratorially in a corner; the lines could have been taken directly out of our mouths. I read a few more phrases, wondering what else you have plundered. Yes, here I am again, awkward and ill at ease in my black and white sequined dress. Am I never to escape you? I skip ahead and read the musings of a young man, hesitating between Cambridge and a career at the bar. Instantly, I feel relieved. It is Thoby to a tee! This is not literature; it is mere journalism. All you have done is reproduce the world you know. It is expertly written, I cannot deny you that, the characters perfectly turned, your sentences full of lyricism and sparkle, yet it does not bring about that change of perspective, that shift in

87

understanding, which is the hallmark of great art. I sit down at the kitchen table. I no longer mind your pilferings. Now that I am sure you have not written a masterpiece, I can read your words with equanimity.

With *To the Lighthouse* it was different. There, for the first time, I felt the full force of your genius. In the intricate balance between composition and vision, in the exquisite execution of each phrase, I knew, despite myself, that you were a consummate artist and that nothing I could do would ever compete. Once again, you had told our story, yet this time you had done so in a way that bridged the gap between biography and art. You had painted Mother and Father with a surety that took my breath away. It was as if, by homing in on certain traits, you could give them to your reader with a directness that made them archetypal as well as vivid, instructive as well as real. You had freed them from the snares of memory and used them to reflect on the deeper issues of human life. You had done all this in prose of such limpidity, such poignancy, that I could only marvel at your gift. You had done more. Through the boldness of your framework, extending and then collapsing time so as to show its impact rather than its passage, you had opened up new possibilities for your art. I began to see equivalent hurdles and prospects in my own work. For once, what you had accomplished was so momentous it advanced us both.

How entangled our lives must seem to anyone outside the skein. Did I sense, when I encouraged Leonard to propose to you and persuaded you to accept him, the life raft I was sending you? I was the carnal sister, you were the intellectual — so the story runs. The truth is rather different. You experienced intimacies in your marriage I could only dream of. Perhaps if I had been able to accept devotion, I, too, might have had my Leonard. There was a flaw, a failing or wound in my nature, that made me indifferent to all that Roger offered. I had a restless desire in me, some deep-seated impulse to pursue what I knew to be impossible, that caused me to spurn the one man who might have helped me succeed. I rejected Roger's care for the dubious challenge of trying to turn aloofness into love. I did not realize that in doing so I was repeating an old pattern.

The figure in the foreground has her back to us. While it is clear that she is the presiding presence in the picture, there is another figure opposite her, which, once we have seen it, barters for our attention. The face of this second figure is solemn, judgmental, domineering. There is something repellent about the downward turn of the mouth. There is a table between the two figures, bare except for some plates and glasses, a jug, a plate of bread. The white linen cloth repels rather than attracts the eye. The figure in the foreground has her head bowed. We cannot see her face. Only the bend of her head, the angle of her arm as she reaches for a plate suggests her powerlessness. We sense that she is unhappy and that she would, if she could, restore harmony and well-being to the scene. There are two children seated with the women round the table. On the left is a small boy, pinioned in his highchair. He watches the women intently. Opposite, her head grouped conspiratorially with the figure at the far end of the table, is the glowering face of a fair-haired girl. She has her legs perched on the bar of her chair and there is no mistaking the look of malicious willfulness in her eyes.

As I reconsider the painting today, I am shocked by its stark-ness. There is no ornament, nothing extraneous, everything is stripped bare. I see the woman's disapproval, the girl's jeal-ousy, the anguish of the figure whose face is hidden from view. I sense Mother's critical detachment, your taut vigilance, my own efforts to placate and win approval. The small boy might be Adrian or one of my sons. Or it might be no one in particu-lar. Art is not life, after all.

I lie on my bed, my face turned toward the wall. I tell my-self I should go down, that everyone will be waiting for me. I have the Christmas meal to attend to, the children's stockings to prepare. Already I can hear carol singers in the hall. I shut my eyes. I cannot hold the pieces of my life in place anymore. Last night, at dinner, Clive sat next to Mary and listed her ac-complishments as if she were a precious object he longed to possess.

I drift in and out of sleep. I remember Stella, showing me how to give substance to my figures by shading round them. Her hand closes round mine, and as she guides my pencil, I see that she is holding something, an object I cannot quite make out. I know I must take it from her and keep it safe. Your face is in front of me now. We are underwater, and I sense that what Stella has given me will keep us afloat. Looking down, I realize what I have in my hand is a mirror. Your fea-tures are distorted by the water but I can read your fear. I hold the mirror out toward you. You understand at once but in-stead of taking the mirror start to swim away. I call after you, surprised by how clearly my voice sounds. I am terrified that if I let you go you will drown. I swim after you, and as I draw level, I grab hold of your shoulder. I thrust the mirror into your hand. The next time I look you are high above me on dry ground.

I am too exhausted to struggle. I shout to you but this time my voice makes no sound. As I sink, I become aware of someone catching me. I open my eyes and see Roger in the water beside me. Perhaps, if I can cling to him for long enough, I will find you and the mirror again.

It is one of those mornings when the sky looks as if it has been scrubbed. I feel chill and out of sorts as we walk past St. Pancras to the Register Office. You are sitting with Leonard in the waiting room. Your hand is tucked in his, and I have the sudden sense that from now on whatever you do will be shared with Leonard before it is confided in me. I feel like a passenger left waving on the shore while the sleek ocean liner sails from view. I clutch Clive's arm as we make our way to an empty seat, grateful for his presence.

The registrar's opening speech is interminable. I stare at Adrian, thinking how like Thoby he looks. Your face is screened by your hat. I cannot tell how you are feeling. When it comes to the exchange of rings I crane forward. I watch Leonard fit the band of gold onto your finger. You turn toward him then and smile, and the look of tenderness in your eyes is unmistakable. I stand up.

"I wonder if I might ask a question?"

There is a moment's silence as heads turn to see who has spoken. The registrar's eyes travel the room, searching for the source of the interruption. When they find me, his brows knit together in an irate furrow. I have no choice but to press on.

"I wish to change my son's name. I would be obliged if you could advise me of the correct procedure."

How long the days seemed while you were away. I thought about you constantly. I found a map and followed your journey, picturing your bus ride to the top of Mount Serrat, the two of you sailing into Marseilles. I saw you breakfasting in unfamiliar dining rooms, planning out your day's excursion. In bed, at night, I imagined you clasped in Leonard's arms.

To distract myself, I decided to work on a self-portrait. I set a mirror next to my easel and stared into it for some time, studying the hairline creases that had appeared in my brow, the slight sag of my jaw. I could not deny the telltale signs of aging.

Then the first letters arrived. Your descriptions of the French countryside enchanted me. Your account of your travel sickness and Leonard's stoic ability to eat pickled gherkins had me holding my sides in mirth. Once I had got over my delight at hearing from you, I searched your phrases for more intimate details. I puzzled over your references to Leonard, uncertain how to read them. Leonard's letters gave me my answer. They were detailed, frank, and unflinching. You appeared to find lovemaking unappealing, Leonard wrote, and he wondered if I had any advice. I replied immediately. I told him you had always been physically unresponsive, especially with men. I told him I did not think he could change you. That day, I worked on my portrait with renewed energy. When I looked in the mirror it seemed to me my face had regained its bloom.

In many ways, Leonard was Mother's apotheosis. A man of action as well as words, he commanded respect. How different things might have been if, instead of persuading him he was not to blame, I had encouraged him to unbend a little. Perhaps, if I had been more generous, I might have helped him find the confidence to explore. As it was, my words confirmed his fears, and steered you toward a sexless marriage. Fate was to punish me for this.

I cannot now recall exactly when I destroyed that self-portrait. Perhaps it was the day Duncan confessed he could never be my lover again. I do not remember; that time is hazy in my mind. I am glad I destroyed it. The rose flush on my cheek, my look of dreamy contentment, were a lie. I had not told Leonard everything.

There is a heron, far out, silhouetted against the gray-blue. The tide has left pools of water amongst the mud and shingle, calm mirrors of cloud. The three of us walk along the estuary, enjoying the sun on our backs. Roger strides ahead while Clive and I dawdle, pausing to watch the birds grub for food. By the time we reach the jetty all the hire boats have gone. Clive and I settle on one of the benches, glad for this opportunity to rest. Clive takes out a book and starts reading. I gaze at the view, the bustle of the fishermen carrying in their catch, the elegant swoop of the gulls diving for remnants of fish. Roger seethes and fumes at the delay. He walks up and down the jetty, trying to persuade the fishermen to rent us a boat. Finally he succeeds and beckons to us in triumph.

The boat is bigger than the hire boats and we make good progress up the estuary. I sit on a cushion in the prow. At first Clive tries to help Roger with the sails but after a series of rebuttals joins me in the prow. Roger stands at the helm, his hair whipped back by the stiff breeze. I see that he is in his element. I lean back on my cushion and stare up at the billowing sails.

"We should turn back." As if to ignore Clive's words, the boat tacks to the right and we shoot forward. Roger's eyes shine with the exhilaration of the speed. Above me, I can see dark twists of cloud banked up against the blue. Suddenly the sails go slack. They hang limp and flapping like wet sheets. Roger tacks to the left but this time we scarcely move.

"The wind's dropped." Roger hauls in the ropes. Clive raises himself onto an elbow.

"We're a hell of a long way out." I sit up in alarm. I realize that we have left the estuary and are out on the open sea. I feel the waves slap the sides of the boat.

"We must drop anchor and wait for the tide to turn." Clive's voice is reassuringly authoritative. "We can't afford to get dragged any further out."

Roger scowls. He draws in the ropes. The sails fill as we swing round and the boat inches forward, but then stops almost immediately as the airstream caused by the sudden change of direction dies. The sails droop.

"What time is the next tide? Did anyone think to look?" This time Roger answers Clive's question.

"Just after midnight."

"Midnight!" I hear the familiar undertone of thwarted pleasure in Clive's protest. "What a bore! I suppose no one packed any food?" He takes out his pipe and a pouch of tobacco. "Whatever induced you to come so far?"

Roger ignores him. I know by the stubborn set of his shoulders that he will not give in to the delay. He begins to wind the ropes back in.

"Confound it, man! Drop the anchor. It's too risky."

The boat veers round and we gain a few feet. Immediately, before we can lose any ground to the outgoing tide, Roger prepares to tack again. His expression announces how it will be. He will battle the elements, wear himself out to the point of exhaustion, rather than admit defeat. Clive sucks on his pipe, sulky as a child at his spoiled day. I know better than to intervene. I have learned the hard way the consequences of trying to chide either man.

I knew it was right the moment I saw it. Symmetrical and comely, with its sloping roof and large windows, it was a child's drawing of a house. I was overjoyed when you asked me to rent it with you. As the agent showed us through the rooms, a sudden memory of our childhood holidays in St. Ives flashed through my mind.

In the country, I reasoned, I would be free. With Clive safely ensconced in London, and Roger visiting only on weekends, I could live once again at my own rhythm. The children would have a garden to play in, and I could return to my work. The fact that we would have a house independently of our husbands seemed to herald a new era.

In Asheham, my days gradually settled into the pattern that suited me. In the mornings I painted, then we gathered for lunch, and in the afternoons I gardened while the boys played hide-and-seek amongst the apple trees or rooted in the flower beds for treasure. There were frequent visitors. I loved the sense of purposeful absorption that emanated through the house as its occupants settled to some pursuit.

It was at Asheham that I first experimented with art outside a frame. It was here that I began to see that painting might be part of life. I discovered the pleasures of transforming the objects I lived with. I copied the frescoes of Fra Angelico onto the peeling plasterwork in my bedroom, created a jungle of color for the boys. I decorated walls and doors, furniture and ornaments, with figures, flowers, abstract patterns. My work broadened as a consequence.

I stare at your letter, then fold it in two and put it back in my pocket. I rest my elbows on the windowsill and look out over the garden. Something about your tone rings false. Julian's head emerges for a moment from behind one of the currant bushes and I wave at him. He grins at me before disappearing back out of sight. I do not understand why you have canceled your visit. I have planned a surprise birthday party for you, and now all my preparations are in vain. I let your phrases beat round my head, trying to catch their hidden message. It is all Leonard: his article for the *Nation*, his rally for the Russians, his government committee. Whichever way I turn your words, their meaning is the same. Leonard takes precedence over me.

Sometimes love comes instantly, with blinding certainty; sometimes it is a sea mist slowly enveloping the view, until one is hard-pressed to remember the features of the shore.

When did I stop seeing Duncan as my brother's lover and begin to fall in love with him myself? I think it was that very first weekend, when Adrian brought him to Asheham, and I watched him painting in the garden. I had never known Adrian with a lover before and the sight was strangely unnerving. I felt a sharp stab of jealousy as I glimpsed the two of them kissing from my studio window.

96

The next morning I set my own easel alongside Duncan's on the grass. I studied him as I mixed my colors. There was an intensity about his concentration that communicated itself. I seemed to see more clearly as I looked past him toward my chosen subject. As I began to paint, our movements fell into the same pattern. There was no rivalry, only the shared sense of a common pursuit. Not since those far-off days with Thoby in the nursery had I felt so at one with another human being. I could not help falling in love.

I push open the bathroom door. Duncan is standing by the washstand, his shaving brush and razor laid out on a towel. He turns and waves at me, a broad smile on his face. I have spent the afternoon pulling weeds from the vegetable garden, and I am tired and yearning for a bath. Duncan lathers soap onto his cheeks, oblivious of my desire. I wait impatiently for a few moments, then, seeing that Duncan has no intention of hurrying his toilette, decide to start filling the bath. I watch the steam rise in lazy coils as I let in the water. My legs and back ache from my exertions and I long to immerse myself in the heat. I take off my shoes and stockings. Duncan's chin is tilted away from me as he wields his razor across the snowy patina of soap. I remove my dress and knickers and let them drop to the floor. I am naked now except for my chemise. I sense Duncan watching me in the mirror. He grins as we make eye contact and brandishes his soap. I hold up mine in reply. Then I lift the skirt of my chemise and pull it over my head. I climb into the bath.

I pad into my bedroom, swathed in towels. I dress in a skirt and blouse I have thrown over the back of my chair. The blouse is creased and there are smears of paint on the skirt but

I am indifferent to such details. I push my hair into a bunch with my hands and cover it with a saffron scarf.

It does not signify, how I look. I have abandoned all attempts to be fashionable. I have irrevocably put aside the ridiculous ordeal of endeavoring to be well dressed. I tie my scarf in a knot and remember the tedium of trying to keep my hair in its cage of pins. Here I dress for comfort.

I go downstairs. There is a fire in the sitting room and I squat in front of it, holding my palms up to the blaze. Duncan is reading on the sofa. Suddenly I want him to put his arms round me more than anything else in the world. I seat myself beside him and lay my head on his lap. He accepts my homage without a word.

There is a shout at the bottom of the stairs.

"Nessa? Come and see this!" Roger's voice slices through the calm. I hold my brush suspended over my picture, praying that the intrusion will pass.

"Nessa! Where are you? You have to come!" Roger's call sounds closer. I hear him climbing the stairs. I duck my head behind my easel, wondering for one idiotic moment if it will screen me from his view. His body fills the doorway.

"There you are! The post has just come. A card from Saxon. He's found the perfect place, a hotel perched halfway up a Swiss Alp. He suggests we catch the first train. He says it's truly inspirational. What do you think?"

I watch a stray leaf that has blown in through the open window circle the strut of my easel and then fall to rest. I do not want to go to Switzerland. I do not want Roger. He reins in his enthusiasm, sensing he has fallen wide of the mark. He waves the postcard at me and gives a conciliatory smile.

"Another time?" His voice struggles to maintain its cheeriness. I know I have hurt him.

"You could go on your own." I venture the suggestion aware that this is not what he wishes.

"No, no, it was just a mad thought. You know how persuasively Saxon writes." Roger is next to me now, his arm near enough to touch. His love is a cloister, suffocating and dull. I cannot help myself. I must break free.

The bowl of fruit sits in the center of the table, a white dish with green apples. Duncan has set his easel in front of mine, so that from where I am standing I can see the back of his head. I long to tuck the thick locks of hair that continually fall into his eyes behind his ears, run my fingers through his dark mane. I watch him looking at the shelves on the other side of the table and wonder if he will include them in his painting. I decide I will ignore them and concentrate on the dish of fruit. I start to block out my design. There is a bottle near the edge of the table and its shadow falls across the apples. I realize there is a relationship between it and the fruit and I keep it in. Duncan has already begun working. His brush dips in and out of his colors. I am slower in my movements. Each choice, each brush stroke is much more a matter of deliberation. We paint until late in the afternoon. I become absorbed in the cadence of the work and for a time forget the outside world. Only Duncan's presence is real. It is as if the two of us have entered a different sphere. Our eyes travel the same raft of light, converge on the same objects.

Suddenly, a cry pierces the stillness. I recognize it instantly. It is Quentin, waking from his nap, hungry and wanting my attention. I wipe my brush. For the first time, I look at what

I have done. My dish and apples are colossal. They are hewn from granite, monumental. I approve. The way they dominate my composition is right. Duncan is still painting. I steal a look at his canvas and am aghast. While my objects are statuesque, almost ugly in their solidity, his are shapely, iridescent. In his picture the fruit and bottle and table are part of an intricate exchange of shadow and light. My eye follows the reiteration of curves that runs from apple to dish to the jars on the shelves. I note the subtle gradations of hue and compare it to my own crude use of color. I know that I am in the presence of a great artist. My sense of mediocrity as I climb the stairs is familiar.

To my surprise, I find you in the boys' room, sitting in the chair by the window with Quentin on your lap. He has stopped crying and is playing with a toy rabbit you have given him. Julian is kneeling on the floor at your feet, listening eagerly to your story. I perch on one of the beds, reluctant to interrupt. You look at me but before we can speak, Julian tugs at your sleeve, urging you to continue. I close my eyes. Your story is about the fairies that play at the bottom of the garden. I remember Mother's tales of the creatures that lived in the old sheep's skull Thoby found washed up on the beach at St. Ives. To calm your fears Mother wound her green shawl round its horns, and as she tucked you into bed said how it was like a mountain, with valleys and flowers and goats running about. I get up and wander to the window. Duncan has finished painting and is smoking in the garden, his back resting against one of the trees. I think how beautiful he looks as he stares up at the sky. When I turn away you are watching me. You gaze to where Duncan is still standing under the tree. It is impossible to conceal my love from you.

⌁

Leonard is waiting for me as the taxi pulls up in front of your house. He comes toward me as I pay the fare. I can see by his face how anxious he is. Ka has already arrived and we hug each other as Leonard lists your symptoms. We decide Leonard and I should consult Savage at once.

I ask to see you first. You are lying in the darkened room and I sit on the bed beside you. You do not repulse me. I feel calmer now that I know the wild rantings Leonard has witnessed are over. I put my hand on your shoulder and make you promise you will try to eat.

We are in Savage's waiting room when Ka phones. Leonard's face goes pale as the nurse hands him the receiver. I guess at once what you have done.

The taxi plunges through crowded streets. We go over the details of Ka's message. As soon as we arrive Leonard throws open the door and hurries inside the house. I follow slowly to your room. I know even before Leonard finds the empty phial that it is pointless trying to wake you.

The doctors work through the night. We are not allowed to see you. I sit on a chair in the drawing room and stare into the fire.

I cannot bear the thought of life without you.

6

THE SUN STREAMS THROUGH THE WINDOW. I SHIFT round in bed and turn to face the light. As I open my eyes I see the russet and gold of the apple leaves outside. I lie still for a moment and listen to the sounds inside the house. All is quiet. I think of Duncan, asleep in the next room. I get out of bed and slide my feet into slippers, wrapping a shawl round my shoulders. The apple trees dance in the breeze outside, a living mosaic. I go downstairs and put the kettle on the hob.

Duncan appears a few minutes after me, his eyes bleary with sleep. He sits on one of the upturned barrels I have commandeered as chairs and catches hold of my hand. I press my lips to his crown, drinking in his unwashed smell, feeling the coarseness of his hair on my cheek. We stay like this for a moment, and I watch the last of the summer swallows swoop for the crumbs I have thrown onto the lawn. Duncan lets go of my hand. This is the signal for me to withdraw. I busy myself with breakfast, fitting the slices of bread onto the prongs of my fork and toasting them over the fire. We eat like peasants, without

plates or cutlery, grinning in complicit pleasure at our sloven-
liness. I look round the shelves and wonder what we can have
for lunch. There are eggs from the farm. Later I will dig pota-
toes and carrots from the garden. We have bacon and plenty
of preserves. I reach up for a jar of jam to go with the toast.
It is strawberry, bottled last summer. I find a spoon and pass
the jar to Duncan. He takes the spoon and sets it next to a
vase of flowers I have picked for the table. I see him studying
the arrangement, taking in its contours and angles, weighing
it as a subject to paint. I look for a second spoon but cannot
find one. Instead, Duncan puts his finger in the jar and lifts it
to my mouth. I lick it clean of the sweet, sticky jam. He dips
his finger back into the jar. Somehow, we will survive the coming war.

There are two figures. On the right, the artist stands before
his easel. I work hard at his pose. It must convey brilliance as
well as industry, sensitivity as well as single-minded purpose.
I make the artist's clothes dark and dramatic. I do not paint
the features of his face. It is his hands that are important, and
I make several attempts to get the angle of them right. I find it
hard to capture their fluidity and freedom. In the end, I leave
them vague, preferring to hint at their skill rather than risk re-
ducing this to a shape. I set the woman kneeling at the artist's feet. She must not detract from his predominant position.
I dress her simply, in a dark skirt and white blouse. Her face,
too, I leave a blank. It is the arch of her head, the bow of her
shoulders as she crouches over her picture that suggests her
connection to the master. The space between the figures is
crucial. It needs to appear both limitless and close. We must

feel that, while his proximity is vital, it is his detachment, the fact that he stands a little apart, that makes it possible for her to work. I opt for bars of color — green, orange, white, mauve, blue — to fill in the space. I paint each of the bands painstakingly. I mute or brighten, add texture and depth. The colors must imply the potency of their relationship, the power of the paintings we do not see.

As I stand back from my canvas to inspect my work I notice something extraordinary. Despite my intention to foreground the artist, it is the rayed background and the luminosity of the kneeling woman that draw the eye. I study my picture more carefully. Where the artist is somber, leaden, the woman radiates life. She is in her element as she paints. The tones of her blouse, the splash of orange on her boot, are in harmony with the vibrant backdrop. I realize I have done a rare thing. I have painted a woman who is happy.

"You're shutting yourself off from reality! You can't just hide your head in the sand and pretend that the war isn't happening!"

I glower. I had hoped you would support my plan of moving out of London and settling permanently in the country. I look at the tiers of Leonard's books on the shelves behind you. From where I am sitting I can make out some of the titles: *Democracy, International Government*. I feel half defiant and half ashamed. I know the seriousness of what is happening.

"But do you really think all this" — I gesture vaguely toward the neat pile of Leonard's papers on the table — "can make a difference? After all, they burned Clive's pamphlet. If anything it seemed to whip up support for the war. Did I tell you

Duncan was showered with white feathers when we walked home from the village last week? It was horrible. Two of the butcher's boys followed us all the way down the street."

I sigh. I have always found politics impossible to understand. I am not even sure I am in favor of women having a vote. It feels so unconnected to the things that matter. Even now, the thought that the countries of Europe are fighting each other seems such madness I find it difficult to comprehend.

"Just because we're not caught up in all the jingoism doesn't mean we should ignore it. Maynard says that since Kitchener's poster all his brightest students at Cambridge have enlisted. At the very least, we need to work out what all these words that decide our fortunes mean."

I look at your notebook lying face down on the floor beside you. I have not forgotten your request to talk to the Richmond Women's Guild. My silence appeases you. When you speak again your voice is gentler.

"Besides, in the end, your art will suffer."

I bristle. This is something I feel passionately about.

"Politics doesn't come into it! When I'm working on a picture what I'm looking for isn't in the world at large. It's in the relationship between the object in front of me and my marks on the canvas. I never know what it will be when I start working, but I always know when I find it. It's the thing that makes sense of all the rest. It might be an echo — a repetition or movement — or it might be a single joining line."

I stop. My old, nagging fear that you will ridicule whatever I say beats in my head. To my surprise, you are listening intently. For the first time I look at you. Though you are still pale after your illness there is something different about you. I gaze at your plump cheeks, the rosy flesh on your neck, the ample curve of your stomach in your lap. A new thought sears my mind.

"You've put on weight!"

You beam, amused by my change of subject.

"Yes. Leonard did not rule an entire Ceylonese province for nothing. If I eat up all my dishes I am given sweets!"

I stare at you, my thought gaining in depth and awfulness.

"Are you pregnant?"

You flush, then look away. I am too alarmed to worry that I may have stumbled into sensitive territory. I press on.

"I thought you had decided . . . Leonard wrote to me . . ."

"What? That he thinks I shouldn't have children. Well, and why shouldn't I? Savage doesn't see any harm in it, and Jean Thomas says that as long as I'm careful it could do me the world of good. Wouldn't you like to be an aunt?"

I gaze at the floor. It has not occurred to me that you might have children.

"What about your illness? Isn't there a danger childbirth could bring it on?" I am pulling obstacles haphazardly out of the air.

"So you are against me too."

Immediately, I feel guilty.

"It isn't that. I don't want you to be ill again, that's all. Pregnancy can be very draining."

Before you can reply, Leonard comes into the room, carrying a tray of tea. He hands the cups round before settling on the sofa beside you. You clear your throat.

"Nessa has decided to decamp to the country. Shall we follow? We'll need room for all the mongooses and mandrills."

I see from your smile that this is your secret game. Leonard clasps his hands together as if they are paws and waggles his head. He cleans imaginary whiskers. Then he cuffs a paw round your neck and pretends to pick insects out of your hair. You nuzzle his hand, lick the inside of his palms. I put my cup back on the tray and stand up.

"I should be going. I said I would meet Duncan at the workshop."

You accompany me to the door. Leonard's preening monkey imitation still stands between us. In the old days you were my pet. As I turn to go you put your hand on my arm.

"The truth is, Ness, if you settle in the country I will miss you very badly."

Duncan and I are in London for one of Maynard's suppers. He waves to us as we enter the restaurant and points to two empty seats at the far end of the table. We seat ourselves obediently on either side of a tall, powerfully built young man. I feel ostracized from Duncan and wish that I could alter my place. Maynard makes a speech to welcome us, then Lytton tells a lewd joke and we all shriek with laughter. The young man does not join in, I notice. He is nervous and fiddles awkwardly with his knife. I am not the only one to observe his shyness. Duncan strikes up a conversation with him, intended to put him at his ease. I sip my champagne, trying not to mind my exclusion. I overhear the young man say that though his name is David his friends call him Bunny. That night he and Duncan become lovers.

I make my own way back to the house. Sitting in the cab, I do not know what I feel. I picture the two men in bed together, mouths opening in mutual hunger, hands ripping at unwanted clothes. I wind my shawl more tightly across my shoulders and rest my head on the window, glad of its solidity. I feel old and alone, an unwelcome intruder on my children's play. The cab slows to a stop and I open the door and climb out. I pay the driver his fare and let myself into the house. Then I go upstairs and lie on the bed without bothering to undress. All I can do now is wait for sleep.

The persistent ringing of the doorbell wakes me. I open my eyes and am astonished to see sunlight flooding through the window. I raise myself onto my elbows and stare in dismay at my evening dress and boots. Then I remember. Before I have time to sift through my feelings, I hear a voice and the sound of visitors being shown into the hall. I hear protests, explanations, footsteps on the stairs. Finally a knock on my door. I am given no opportunity to reply. Duncan bursts into the room, his smile radiant, and settles himself on my bed. Bunny follows sheepishly in his wake. My anger boils to the surface. Duncan leans over and covers my protests with kisses. Soon I am smiling too. Then we are cradling each other and laughing, and I know that despite what has happened nothing can destroy our bond. Duncan reaches out his arm and pulls Bunny onto the bed beside us.

It is Duncan's idea that Bunny should sit for us. I hang back while Duncan leads him into the room I use as a studio. I busy myself with my easel as Duncan fusses over the details of Bunny's position, trying him in a standing pose, then on a chair, opening and closing the curtains to adjust the light. All the time I sense how impatient Duncan is to start working. When at last we begin to paint, the intensity of Duncan's gaze as he studies Bunny creates a pulse of emotion between the two men that seems to fill the room. I force my eyes to my canvas and grip my brush. If I am going to complete this picture I need to disregard my feelings.

Afterward, when we compare the two portraits, I shrug mine off as a failure. Where Duncan's is the study of an attractive, sexually potent young man, mine is the caricature of a flaccid, pasty-faced boy. There is magnetism and vibrancy in Duncan's working of Bunny's naked torso, energy and tenderness in his rendering of the face. In mine, the planes of color clash with each other, crude blotches of pink, lemon, brown. The bars of green I have mixed into my flesh tones give a sickly sheen to Bunny's skin. His eyes are mere dots, hinting at weakness, self-ishness, even greed. I realize I have painted my jealousy.

I write to Bunny. I lay the sheet of paper flat on the table and pick up my pen. It is not so difficult. I am only framing words, after all. Words cannot hurt, cannot pierce and lacerate the flesh, pulverize one's equilibrium and sense of self. I am invit-ing Bunny to come and live with us. I dangle descriptions of the house and garden, the loveliness of the apple trees in blos-som on the lawn, promise delicious meals, the tranquility to write. I extol the virtues of the new water system, tell him what a paradise the orchard will be for his bees. I woo him with as-surances of how badly he is missed.

I read my letter through, surprised by my capacity to lie. Duncan is pacing backward and forward in front of the fire. He has a blanket over his wet clothes, his hair drips in sodden tangles. He is bitter and impatient and rails against the rain. He reminds me of a lion I saw once with Father, patrolling his cage at the zoo. I remember thinking how terrible his fate was, to be forever dreaming of escape. I sign my letter and seal it in an envelope. I put my coat and hat on to walk to the post, despite the rain. I know that if Bunny does not come soon Duncan will leave.

You stand by the fireplace and study the clusters of fruit I have painted onto the ugly surround. Already the paint is beginning to peel, my shapes buckling in the heat. The remains of last night's party are still on the table, our costumes scattered over the chairs. I see you look at the wool wig and papier-mâché breasts that were Duncan's disguise. Hastily, I sweep the clothes over my arm and clear the table. It is almost lunchtime and Duncan and Bunny are not yet up. I think about the strict work rota you keep to with Leonard and feel ashamed. I know that normally by this time you have written several hundred words. You sit on one of the chairs I have emptied and I think how inconsequential my life must seem to you. Through the open window, I can hear Julian and Quentin playing in the garden. They have filled an old bath with water and are taking it in turns to splash each other, squealing and giggling at the cold. I realize that in a few minutes they will tear into the room, scattering clothes and wet towels as they seize on their next game. I resolve to ignore my throbbing head and take the situation in hand.

"So you have decided to rent the house. I must say I think it's an excellent idea. It's a sound property. And this way you'll have the choice between London and the country."

"Yes. Leonard thinks it will do me good to be out of London."

I find it impossible to tell from your reply whether or not you share Leonard's view. As I had predicted, Julian and Quentin burst into the room, naked except for some streaks of makeup left over from the party. Julian slows as he sees you, then hurtles toward you. To my surprise, you laugh at his wild appearance and allow him to root in your pockets for sweets. When he finds one, you make a show of trying to snatch it from him, feigning vexation as he dodges you and shoots for the door. I wait for peace to settle.

"I'm sorry. We were all up far too late last night. We let the boys dress up with us and they are still very excited."

"So I see. Was it a family party?"

"No, at least . . . Bunny's birthday. It was Duncan's idea that we should wear fancy dress."

Though I work to keep my voice even, I hesitate as I say Bunny's name. You look at me.

"Did you organize the party?"

"Bunny . . ." I stop in confusion.

"Ness? What is it?"

I blurt it all out. I cannot help myself. I have to tell someone.

"After the boys had gone to bed Duncan fell asleep on the sofa. We'd all had quite a bit to drink and Bunny and I decided the best thing would be to leave him there. I found a blanket and turned out the lights and Bunny and I went upstairs together. As I turned to go to my room, Bunny caught hold of my arm and thanked me for the party. I wished him many happy returns and he kissed me on my cheek. But the kiss did not stop where it should have done and I had to . . . extricate myself."

"And you didn't want him?"

"No, of course not! I know how it must seem to you . . . as if I am nothing . . . but sleeping with Bunny would have felt like a violation."

I burst into tears. I no longer care what you think of me.

The failure of my life is set out for you to see. You get up and kneel in front of me.

"Darling, don't cry."

You pull my head onto your shoulder and rock me gently to and fro.

"You don't really believe what you're saying. Just look around you."

I lift my head.

"What? The children are out of control, the house is falling down round my ears, my paintings don't sell."

You kiss my face.

"Don't you know how much I love coming here? Don't you know I'd give up writing tomorrow if I could exchange it for one tiny piece of all this?"

I look at you incredulously. You gesture toward the hearth, the ripe peaches and apricots I have worked round it. Your hand finds the pattern in the stem and leaves, connecting the fruit, weaving the chaos of my decoration into shapes. I hear Julian and Quentin playing happily again in the garden. Soon, Duncan will appear, and I will go into the kitchen and see to lunch. Gradually, the scraps of my life — the debris from the party, the children's discarded clothes, my half-finished fireplace — coalesce into a whole. You have made a painting.

"Go on, I dare you." Marjorie says the words as if she is throwing down a gauntlet. Duncan pokes me in the ribs.

"Go on, Nessa! It will be fun!" His eagerness surprises me.

"Very well." I seat myself on the silk cushions Marjorie has laid out next to her. She takes hold of my hand and turns it palm upward.

"Are you comfortable?"

I nod. Marjorie closes her eyes and takes several deep breaths. I stare at a jeweled brooch of two fighting dragons she has pinned to her dress. Marjorie opens her eyes and studies my hand. She has a peacock feather in her hair that quivers whenever she moves.

"You have a strong lifeline. Although it is broken in places, suggesting illness, you will nonetheless live to an advanced age." Marjorie's tone is seductive. Despite my skepticism, I am curious to know what she will say next.

"You will have one, two, three, four . . . no . . . three children." My heart skips a beat and I wonder if Marjorie has heard my secret prayer. I look at Duncan, who I see is listening intently to the prediction.

"You will love and be loved passionately, but" — here Marjorie raises my hand even closer to her face, as if to check the accuracy of her forecast — "this will not necessarily be the same person." I can feel my breath coming hot and fast. Duncan frowns.

"What about her character? Surely there are some clues." I sense his desire to change the subject. Marjorie peers at my palm again.

"Secretive. Taciturn. Jealous. You are hiding something . . . a wound, perhaps?" I shiver, suddenly exposed. I snatch my hand away and stand up.

"Come on, Duncan. It's your turn. Let's hear what secrets you are hiding."

The war began to make itself felt. Maynard brought terrifying stories of zeppelins from the Treasury; Rupert was killed in the fighting in Turkey. Compulsory conscription edged closer.

Duncan's father agreed to lease him a farm in the hope he might be spared from active service when it came.

We were unprepared for the dereliction we found. The fruit trees had been left unattended, and many of the fields were so clogged with weeds that in places it was difficult to walk. The hencoops were rotten and the hens that remained had taken refuge in a disused barn. A few undernourished sheep huddled in a corner of the farmyard, disconsolately pulling wisps of straw from a disheveled hayrick. The whereabouts of the cows was a mystery we never managed to solve.

While Duncan and Bunny pruned the fruit trees, I set to work on the house. I distempered over the peeling wallpaper, took down the mildewy chintzes left by previous tenants. I dyed curtains and cushion covers and hung our pictures on the walls. I went through each room in turn, creating spaces to live and work in. When things were as comfortable as I could make them, I helped Duncan and Bunny with the farm.

We all agreed that the fields needed plowing, yet though we found a serviceable plow in one of the outbuildings no one would lend us a horse. Day after day Bunny trudged round the adjoining farms. The story was always the same: all the horses were in use. Finally I suggested we try pulling the plow ourselves. It was backbreaking work, and after only a few hours we had to admit defeat. We limped back to the house exhausted.

And yet. There was a purpose and serenity to our days. Hearing the children play hide-and-seek in the garden, it was easy to forget the fighting overseas. I set up a studio in the least dilapidated of the barns and painted the blossom in the orchard. As we gathered the apples and pears, I felt a sense of fulfillment. Our queer triangle seemed a haven of sanity compared to the war. My silent wish, as I opened my eyes each morning, was that nothing should disrupt our peace.

When the house became too cold, we moved into a barn where the stove was more reliable. I slept in a box bed that had been built into the wall, and Duncan and Bunny spread rugs on the floor. I sent the children to stay with Clive and for weeks on end we saw no one. While the two men tended the animals, I concocted meals from whatever ingredients I could find. When I could, I worked. I painted the skeletons of the trees, the thick cocoon of snow that for a short time effaced the world. I sensed that if I waited long enough things would right themselves. As we huddled together during the dark winter evenings, the taut coil of Duncan's desire began to unravel. Each morning, I gazed out over the frozen landscape and looked for signs of spring.

When Bunny first announced his intention to leave, I greeted the news like a welcome liberation. It was what I had dreamed of for so long. Yet I knew I had to be careful. I hung Duncan's portrait of him above the fireplace when we were at last able to move back into the house, as a reminder of the place he had held. I wrote to him with our news. Bunny responded with details of his work in France, the terrible plight of the refugees he was helping. Duncan listened in silence as I read his letters out loud.

It is New Year's Eve. You are wearing a dove-gray dress with a lace collar and trim. Leonard presides, handing round drinks. I sit opposite you and try to make you laugh with anecdotes of my Christmas at Garsington. You look tired. Your eyes have that opaque look I have come to fear. I want to reach across and put my arm round you. Instead, I describe the pantomime

116

we all took part in; Ottoline's extraordinary disguises. I ask how you are. Before you can say, Leonard is upon us, fussing in case you are tired. You shake your head when he suggests you should go to bed. I watch you rally, fire a question at Maynard, then one at Clive. Leonard hovers for a moment, then seeing he cannot prevail, resumes his role as host. Inevitably, the conversation turns to the war.

"So you think it will come, then." No one is fooled by Clive's matter-of-fact tone. We all lean forward to catch Maynard's reply.

"Yes. It will be announced in the course of the next few days. Compulsory conscription for all men between eighteen and forty-one not in sole charge of dependents."

There is a moment's silence during which we each make our private calculations. It is Duncan who breaks it.

"I will simply refuse. What is the worst they can do to me?"

"Imprisonment. Forced labor. With all that this can mean." Duncan changes color at Maynard's words. I have a sudden image of Duncan in prison: his spirit broken, unable to paint.

"There must be alternatives, surely?" It is the first time Bunny has spoken. He gulps down the drink Leonard gives him.

"Yes. One can apply for exemption. Usually on health grounds. There is some provision for conscientious objectors. It's limited, though, and dependent in the first instance on local tribunal."

Clive groans.

"We all know what that means. Bigots whose only motive is self-interest."

Duncan jumps on a chair and mimes the part of a malicious magistrate, rolling his eyes in mock pleasure as he conducts

117

an imaginary flogging. We all join in his charade. Clive sings "Rule, Britannia," while Maynard lists increasingly absurd reasons for the refusal of exemption from active service. Bunny slumps in his chair and pretends to snore, an indolent, overfed judge. Leonard plays the puzzled general, peering at an invisible map and scratching his head as he tries to locate his troops. Even you rub your hands in feigned glee as you contemplate the carnage. We clap and cheer as the sketch plays itself out, grateful for the relief it has brought. The seriousness of this next stage in the war is lost on no one.

There were two hearings. At the first, which I attended, the farmers who made up the jury unanimously rejected both Duncan's and Bunny's pleas for objector status. For a few terrible weeks, prison seemed inevitable. I did everything I could think of to keep Duncan safe. I wrote to anyone I hoped might be able to influence the case, asking them to intervene on our behalf. In the end, the second hearing was won thanks to Maynard's testimony. Duncan's and Bunny's appeals were upheld on condition that they engaged in work of "national importance."

That night, the three of us opened the last of the wine Bunny had brought back with him from France. We lay shoulder to shoulder on the mat in front of the fire, gazing up at the ceiling. We were drunk, and the dark that pressed against the windows seemed to offer protection. Staring up into the shadows, Bunny conjured fields of ripening corn, orchards laden with fruit. Duncan added prolifically laying hens and flocks of well-fed sheep, while I, in turn, created sackfuls of vegetables from the garden, bunches of drying herbs, pots of preserves. Together we fashioned paradise, bodies interlaced, until the war became no more than a distant inferno, an insane conflagration that would flare and burn and eventually fade.

The next morning I got up early, leaving Duncan and Bunny asleep. I dressed quickly and packed my bag with half a loaf of bread, two apples, and some of the remains of the cheese from our feast the night before. It was still dark as I took my bicycle from the outhouse and wheeled it over the grass to the lane. I thought about our closeness as we lay before the fire, our shared resolution to survive. I felt the power come back into my limbs as I pedaled down the lane. The cool air revived me, gave me a steeliness of purpose. I knew what I had to do. To satisfy the tribunal, Duncan and Bunny could not act as their own employers. I had to find them work.

At the station, I bought a ticket and waited on the platform for the train. I tried to recall my brief introduction to Mr. Hecks at Lewes market. When the train came I lifted my bicycle into the guard's van and made my way to the second-class seating. I was determined to plead our case. It had to be done in person; a letter would not do so well.

I took a deep breath as I stopped my bicycle at the farmyard gate and dismounted. I rested it against the low stone wall and walked toward the house. The front door was slightly ajar. I rang the bell and a maid in a dirty apron appeared. I quickly explained why I had come. Without saying a word, the maid pointed toward an adjacent barn. I hurried toward it. Though it was only dimly lit inside, Mr. Hecks remembered me from our meeting. Yes, he replied in answer to my eager questions, he would be glad of two extra pairs of hands and promised to give Duncan and Bunny work. All I had to do now was find us a house.

∽

It was you who first told me about it. Leonard had seen an advert in the local paper and the two of you had been to look at it. It seemed to have everything I needed, and if I took it, you wrote coaxingly in your letter, we would be within visiting distance of each other again. Yet the first time I saw it all I noticed were its faults.

Something drew me back. The sky was cloudy as I cycled up the rough track, and this time, as I went in through the gate, the setting struck me. There was a pond in front of the house, shaded by trees. As I looked, the sun broke from behind the clouds, turning the white flowers on the clematis silver. The house had a red tiled roof and windows that were too big for it, as if the builder had mistaken the proportions.

A Mr. Stacey let me in. There was no denying the light that poured in through the vast windows, and my heart began to quicken as he escorted me through the rooms. There was ample accommodation, and I sketched out a plan in my mind. This could be a bedroom for Clive, this a study for Maynard; there were rooms for Duncan and the children, a studio for myself. A side door led to the garden proper. Here marigolds, poppies, foxgloves, and cornflowers grew in wild profusion. I seemed to hear the carefree shouts of the children playing among them. I imagined Duncan painting on the terrace, guests strolling about the lawn. In the center of it all, I saw myself, vital, enabling, beloved. I made up my mind. I turned to Mr. Stacey and informed him that I would take the house on a long lease.

7

I WIPE MY BROW WITH MY HAND AND LEAN BACK ON
my haunches. The earth is warm to my touch. I look up and
see clouds chasing each other against the blue. I try to trace
the mythical beasts and castles I glimpsed in them as a child.
I pick up my runner beans and gently ease the young seed-
lings from their tray. I place them in the holes I have prepared,
packing the soil over the roots. Their delicate tendrils shiver in
the air. Soon they will curl round the sticks I have planted and
pull themselves up toward the light.

Settling into Charleston has not been easy. The house has
no running water or electricity, and many of the rooms remain bare despite the furniture Maynard has sent us. I have
distempered the walls, mixing Indian red and cobalt to soften
the whiteness, but apart from this I have had little time to decorate. With the shortages from the war increasing and Duncan and Bunny out at work each day my priority is the garden. Sometimes, as I look up from my weeding or planting, I

imagine one of the rooms as if it is a bare canvas and try out a design in my mind. I plan a frieze of blue and yellow moons above Duncan's window, and a contrasting echo of green and brown circles below the sill. I find a stick and sketch a vase of lilies and poppies for his door. I wonder if my flowers are a recompense for all the plants I have pulled up in the garden. Food is in such short supply that we need every inch of soil to grow vegetables and fruit.

I survey my work. I have told Clive I do not want to send the boys away to school and that I will educate them here. I have taken on a governess, and extra pupils to help with the cost. I dig up a dandelion that has seeded itself amongst the carrots. I am worried about Julian. Quentin applies himself readily enough to lessons, but Julian sabotages whatever I ask him to do. He fidgets whenever my back is turned and appears jealous of any attention I give to the other children. Only yesterday when I helped Anna-Jane with her still life he knocked the dish of fruit to the floor.

I unwrap the plants Duncan has brought up from the farm. There is still so much to do. I dig the holes for the peas with my fingers, my nails drilling the malleable earth. I look beyond the garden to the horizon. Firle Hill stands before me, its great curving mound deserted. There is no one I can confide in. I am like the captain of a ship who must bear all the consequences of his actions alone. Sometimes, as I lie in bed at night, I seem to hear the intermingled breathing of all those who depend on me. I must sail my ship to safety. A wasp buzzes round my face and I flap it away. I have not had time to bury the rotting fruit from last year's crop that lies heaped in the orchard. I finish my peas and wipe my soiled hands on my skirt. It is time to give the children their French lesson. Then

I will prepare a soup for when Duncan and Bunny return ravenous and exhausted from their work. I stand up, and as I do so, become aware of a sudden distant booming. I realize with a start that it is the sound of gunfire. This is the first time I have heard the war. My anguished cry sends the rooks in the elms into frenzied flight.

You visit with Leonard. I am in the sitting room, painting the tiles round the fireplace when you arrive. I have spent the morning gardening and my clothes are stained with mud. I have given the children a half-day's holiday, and as I work I listen to Julian and Quentin storming the remains of the shrubbery with homemade guns. I wipe my hands hastily on a rag. You are wearing a deep-blue dress with a wide neckline that I recognize as one of the Omega designs from Roger's workshop. I clear a space for the two of you to sit down and disappear into the kitchen to make tea.

When I return you are alone, examining the tiles I have been painting. I place the tray of tea on the floor between us.

"Leonard has gone to find the boys," you say by way of explanation. You gesture toward one of the tiles. "Is this meant to be the sea?"

I stare at the image you point to, trying to dismiss my nagging thought that I should go after Leonard and round up the boys. I know he believes I am too indulgent toward them, that they would benefit from tighter control.

"I suppose I was thinking about the sea, though of course it was the color and pattern I had most clearly in mind."

You consider my answer.

"So if you weren't thinking about a particular seascape, what did you intend this mark to be here?" You draw your finger

123

along a straight black line down the center of the tile. "I had assumed it was a lighthouse."

I look at the line. I remember painting it, sensing that the swirls of blue required an anchoring point.

"I'm not sure I meant anything in particular by it, though of course I've no objection to you seeing it as a lighthouse." I pick up the pot and pour two cups of tea. You continue to examine the tile.

"But if it isn't a lighthouse — or indeed anything specific — why is it there?"

I add milk to the tea and pass you one of the cups. There is a bloodcurdling shriek from outside the window and I glance up. The garden appears deserted.

"The blue needed it, the pattern needed it. It gives the eye something to rest on."

You allow me no time to draw breath.

"So you want to include your onlooker?"

"Of course. Though I'm not sure I'm predominantly thinking about my audience as I paint."

"I'm glad to hear it. Though actually I worry I don't think enough about my reader. When I write I do so because it gives me an opportunity to go further into something — a chance to enter what I would otherwise be excluded from. Whereas you — if I understand you correctly — must confront the opposite problem. You are already inside, and your challenge is to find a point of perspective for those who are outside your work."

I stand up.

"You make too much of what I'm doing. I paint first and foremost . . . so as not to feel."

I have said enough. I pick up my shawl and resolve to look for the boys. Before I can do so Leonard comes in from the garden.

"Did you find them?" My words jerk out too quickly. Leonard's face sets in a frown as he shakes his head. I sense his disapproval of the boys' unruly play. I pour a third cup of tea as he seats himself next to you. He winds your scarf more closely about you, and his fingers linger on your neck. You catch hold of his hand and kiss his palm. I peer down at my cup. The thought of the solitary bed I must go to each night rises to haunt me. There is a rattle of stones against the window. I look up and see a face.

"Thoby!"

You stare at me, an expression of vexed disbelief on your face. I get up and cross to the window. Quentin appears in the doorway, his hair disheveled, a wooden sword in his hand. His brother troops in behind him.

"Good. There you are. Julian. Come in and have some tea." It is only as I say his name that I realize my mistake. Julian was Thoby's first name, and in my dismay I have confused the two. You have never approved of my wish to call Julian after Thoby. The boys file in and settle themselves on the floor beside you. They spar and jostle for your attention. You tease them about their wild appearance, find sweets for them in your bag. They laugh and clap and hang on your every word. I begin to fear they are growing away from me.

I say very little for the remainder of your visit. You tell a story, and the boys sit tame and quiet beside you. I notice a ring I have not seen before on one of your fingers. When the time comes for you to leave, I watch you walk down the drive, your arm tucked in Leonard's, the boys dancing in attendance behind you.

I ask you to sit for me. Somehow I justify the time. I set my easel in the garden, sensing that my task will be easier if I suggest you simply daydream in a chair. I know how you hate being looked at. I block out the frame of your chair, the contours of your body. I work the warm sienna of your dress, the flame of your scarlet tie. As I paint, my feeling of isolation starts to recede. All the hurts and disappointments I have had to bear gradually diminish, until what I am left with is the thing before me and the rhythmic movement of my hand. I think of Mother in her deck chair in the garden at St. Ives, her eyes closed as she allowed herself a few minutes' peace after lunch. My brush restores the caress of hands, the longed-for shelter of loving arms. I fill out the brim of your hat, the band of your hair framing your face. I form the arch of your nose, the bow of your mouth. When the features of your face are done I stop and examine the effect. I have failed. I pick up my knife and scrape the paint clear. I gaze at your closed eyelids, the back of your head resting against the chair. I wash the entire oval of your face in a flesh tone. I look again. This time your expression is a blank. I set my brush aside. I have painted what you are to me.

The winter is bitterly cold. In the mornings, I hurry out of bed, wrapping myself in an old blanket as I make my way to the kitchen where I prepare breakfast for Duncan and Bunny. I set the kettle on the hob and slice the bread. Then I pack whatever food I can find into two canvas bags for their lunch. It is still dark as Duncan and Bunny stumble into the kitchen, forcing chilblained fingers and toes into gloves and boots. The water in the basins I have left on the floor to catch the drips from the leaking roof has frozen. Our pipes are frozen too. We will be forced to spend the morning tramping across fields with our buckets to collect water from the spring. They are harvesting turnips up at the farm and I wonder how they will dig the ground. I pour the boiling water into the teapot, squeezing the leaves with a spoon against the side in a vain attempt to produce a stronger brew. There is very little tea left and we have had no coffee for weeks. Duncan accepts the cup of steaming tea gratefully. He looks exhausted. He is not as strong as Bunny and the months of hard labor are beginning to exact their toll. His eyes are swollen from lack of sleep and his skin has a papery appearance, like old documents. I long to take him in my arms, to lay him in my bed and hold him while he sleeps. Instead, I rake the fire, set the places for the children's breakfast. When Duncan and Bunny have finished eating I kiss them goodbye, watching from the door as they trudge down the lane until the cold forces me back inside.

The war edges closer. Its madness infiltrates the house. It steals through doors, seeps between crevices, invisible, contagious, evil. Julian hits his governess so violently I must apply a cold compress to her face. I can no longer find reliable help in the house. One morning it is ten o'clock before Emily appears, and when I reprimand her for her lateness, she announces her decision to leave. She can earn better wages, so she tells me, making munitions for the war. The food shortages intensify. Duncan is now so tired that he regularly falls asleep over his evening meal. Often Bunny and I end up carrying him to his bed. I long to sleep too. I long to pull the covers up over my head and wake in a different place, somewhere life is not such a struggle.

I lie in bed and listen to the wind in the trees, trying not to hear the pounding of the guns across the channel, or the slow tread of Bunny's pacings outside my door. Still he has not given up his desire to sleep with me. I close my eyes and hope his offensive will pass.

There is a sudden shout. I sit up, and for a moment I do not know if the sound is real or if it is inside my head. I hear a thud and another shout and then another. I pull the cover from my bed and run to the door. It is dark on the landing and I stand and listen. The shouts are coming from the room at the far end. I push open the door. On the floor, many-limbed and monstrous in the candlelight, are the naked writhing bodies of Duncan and Bunny.

"I'll teach you!" There is a suppressed howl as Bunny forces himself on top of Duncan. The bodies interlock.

"You bastard!" Duncan's voice is tight with pain. I see Bunny's fist flail blows on Duncan's chest. I take the cover from round my shoulders and fling it over the two men. My action has the desired effect.

"Get up." I pull the cover away. "Now."

Bunny stumbles to his feet, sweating and defensive, blood oozing from a cut on his lip. Duncan remains motionless on the floor. I can hear the strain of his breathing. Slowly he pulls himself into a sitting position. I help him to his feet. He puts his arm round my shoulder, swaying as he tries to regain his balance. I lead him back to my room.

I know better than to ask what the fight was about. I climb into bed alongside Duncan and cradle him in my arms. He weeps as he buries himself in my flesh. When his seed pumps into me I wonder if it is me or Bunny he is thinking of.

Mary agrees to pose for me. I no longer mind that she has become Clive's lover. I make her stand with her head bowed, gaze lowered to the floor. Her hair is tied in a single plait. At first I am uncertain where her hands should go. I try them in front of her, then resting by her side. Neither position is right; the stance is too open, too inviting. I ask Mary to raise her hands to her plait, as if she is still in the process of fastening it. The gesture works. It has the right blend of introspection and concern for surface appearances. I block out the rest of her figure quickly, and turn my attention to the bathtub. After some deliberation I decide to upend the tub slightly, breaking its rotundity by introducing a flat line at the base. My brush lingers over its contours. I concoct a silvery gray for the sides, built up with streaks of black, white, turquoise, pale pink. I pause before I paint the bottom, hesitating between the colors I have used for the sides and the rich bronzes and gold I plan for the floor. In the end, I combine the two. I stand a vase in the arched space I create behind the bathtub. I pick carmine shadowed with russet, a gash against the serenity. I think for a long time about what flowers to put in the vase. I picture a display of leaves from the garden, purple and yellow flag irises, lacy coils of the hydrangea in bloom along the wall. None seems right and I reject them all. Instead, I repeat the curve of the arch to make three separate stems, two falling to the right, one to the left. I mold the oval of a tulip at the end of each stem, using the reds I have already mixed for the vase. At the last moment I make the solitary flower to the left a pale lemon. I do not know why I do this, except that I sense the need to divide the flowers, so that while two are in close proximity, the other stands estranged and aloof.

I return to my figure. I am satisfied with her head and hands, but the white chemise I have dressed her in is too soft. I decide to remove the chemise and paint the figure nude. I consider asking Mary to pose for me again, but as I begin to define breasts and shoulders I realize I can invent the lines I need. With no real-life model to influence me, I build the flesh tones from the gold and ocher I have prepared for the floor. As the figure merges into the background, it simultaneously retreats from the viewer and separates itself from the circle of the tub.

I leave the canvas on my easel for several weeks. Something in me is reluctant to let it go. I find myself returning to it, stopping and staring, sometimes for an hour at a stretch. I am drawn by the figure's stillness, as well as the contradiction between the enveloping potential of the tub's contours and the unyielding chasm at its heart. I am intrigued that whereas the silvery gray I used for the sides initially invited contemplation, the tints now have an iciness to them caused by the opulent gold of the floor. At length I take the canvas down and parcel it up to send to Roger to sell. I write him a letter, telling him I think my composition balances realism with abstraction. I do not confess how true I think it is.

"You've no right to be jealous!" Roger's words are addressed to Duncan, who has pulled a stool up close to the fire and is staring miserably into the flames.

"I agree. It's the attraction of the sexes. Bunny and Barbara. What could be more natural, after all?" Clive lounges on the sofa, puffing at his pipe. I am in the armchair, knitting. I cock an ear to the conversation.

"Are you saying that love between men isn't as strong as the love between men and women?" I hear the fraught note of anguish in Duncan's voice. Clive waits a moment before he replies.

"What I think is that the differences are important. Love flourishes in the gap."

"That isn't love!" Roger leans forward in his chair. "Anyway, why shouldn't another man constitute sufficient difference from oneself? If difference *is* the magic ingredient."

"Different or not, I wish I'd never set eyes on him!" Duncan's tone now is petulant. He reaches for a log from the basket and tosses it on the fire. The flames leap.

"I remember the first time I fell in love. I was seventeen, eighteen, perhaps." We settle to hear Roger's story. Even Duncan looks round from the blaze. "It was a woman I had seen many times before, without incident. Then one day, as I passed her in the street, I noticed a curious expression on her face. Her eyes were lit up, almost belligerent. She looked both pleased with herself and as if she were searching for something — as if she had just eaten a delicious meal and was still famished. After that, I couldn't stop thinking about her. I kept imagining those devouring eyes turned on me. By the time I saw her again it was too late, she was veiled in my fantasy. I could no longer see her as she was. I was hopelessly in love, yet it was my illusion about her that made me fall, rather than anything she said or did." Roger's words tail into silence. We each sit thinking about our experiences of love. Clive is the first to speak.

"There is a kind of illusion. But I don't believe the illusion is without truth. There has to be something in the person you fall in love with that kindles the illusion, as you call it. Some quality you see and respond to, something that merits all the feelings you lavish upon them."

Duncan groans. "You're making it too abstract! Of course it's both those things — your own intrinsic nature and the way you perceive the other person, the way what you see dovetails with your own character. But there are also raw emotions — hopes, frustrations, needs . . ."

Clive raises himself to a sitting position. "I for one would never go to bed with someone I felt didn't want to go to bed with me."

"From the way I understand it," Roger interrupts him, "the problem is not that Bunny doesn't want to go to bed with Duncan. The problem is that Bunny also wants to go to bed with Barbara."

"If there were only Barbara!" Duncan's joke falls flat.

"Nevertheless" — Clive raises his pipe, reluctant to let go of his train of thought — "there has to be reciprocity. Otherwise one is laying oneself open to pain. It becomes degrading too — to want and want and never to have that want satiated. It eats away at you. In the end, you can't even see how humiliating it is."

I am not sure when I stop listening. I am not even certain I have remembered the conversation accurately or if it is my own tortured brain supplying the phrases. All I know is that at some point I fold my knitting and quietly slip out of the room. I climb the stairs and wish that the thin sliver of moon I can see hanging outside the landing window would pick me up and spirit me away. I go into my room and lie on my bed. I bury my head in the pillow, letting the coolness of the cotton seep into my brow. Images flicker on the closed screen of my eyelids. The drawn lines of Duncan's face as he knelt before the fire, your arm tucked in Leonard's as you disappeared down the drive with the boys dancing beside you. I curl my fingers into fists, clasp my legs to my chest. How long I remain like this I cannot say.

There is a tap and a light in the doorway. Reluctantly I open my eyes. Duncan kneels on the floor beside my bed and strokes my hair.

"Nessa." His voice pulses with remorse. "I do love you. You know that."

I cannot bear to answer. Instead, I grasp his hand and bring it to my lips. I know that now, if I ask him, he will come into my bed. I pull back the cover. We are gentle with each other and when we have finished I lie motionless in his arms. I gaze at the moon through the uncurtained window, thankful for this truce.

I lean over the compartments of type and watch while you select the letters. You place each letter upside down at the bottom of the tray. When you come to the end of the line you set a strip of lead above the letters, positioning it carefully before you start the next row.

"It's actually rather restful, once you get used to it," you say as you show me the finished phrase. I try to decipher the upside-down words. I marvel at the swiftness of your fingers as you tip the letters out of the tray and return them to their separate boxes. I envy your look of calm absorption.

"Of course," you continue, "we had a terrible time getting the machine to work. All we had was an instruction manual and Leonard's rudimentary knowledge of mechanics."

I picture you and Leonard poring over the manual together, hugging each other in triumph as you remove the first printed page from the press.

"So what sort of books will you print?" I ask.

You laugh.

"That all depends on how quickly we can master the art! At the moment we're thinking about one of Katherine's stories and a small collection of poems by Tom. Perhaps some essays. We're starting with two stories, one by Leonard and one by me."

I yawn. I get up from the table and walk over to the open window, resting my arms on the sill. You call me back.

"Carrington has done some woodcuts for us. I didn't realize how talented she is until Lytton showed us some of her work. We've already had a go at printing them. Would you like to see?"

You hand me a sheet of paper with four printed images on it. Their crisp, bold lines impress me.

"How do you plan to use the woodcuts?" I ask, seating myself back at the table.

"We can put them on the dust jacket, as a frontispiece, inside the text. The possibilities are endless."

"You mean you can print the woodcuts alongside the words?"

"Yes. It's not that difficult to do. Once I've worked out the space I need for the image, I simply set the type around it."

I ask if I can take the printed page home with me. That night, when everyone is in bed, I get out the story you sent me. This time, as I read, I visualize the garden you describe so evocatively. Now, as my eyes travel the lines of your prose, my mind races with ideas. I find paper and charcoal. I work flowers, stems, leaves round your words. I sketch the two women talking in the garden, their hats tilted at an angle as they exchange confidences. I draw quickly, excitedly. Soon I have covered your story with my pictures. On some pages I design a simple border, on others I concoct more elaborate illustrations, images from the garden, decorative patterns. In the morning, I parcel up the story and send it back to you. I add a note saying that I enjoyed working on it. As I go about my chores I sense my spirits reviving. I see the printed book of your story with my woodcuts prominent on each page.

So. I am to have another child. Despite all the tribulations of my love for Duncan it will have produced this. I prop the mirror against the bed and stand before it. As yet, there is little to detect. A slight swelling in my breasts, the faint puckering of the skin around the nipples, a decided roundness in my belly. For the moment the baby is a mirage, no more real than a wish. I raise my eyes to my face and see a tiny figure reflected in my pupils. I think of you, bent over your writing table, drafting your new novel. You have accomplished so much more than me. Suddenly, I sense an inner, subterranean shift. I let my hand rest on my belly. The figure in my eyes gleams.

I decide to have the baby at home. As Christmas approaches I make my plans. The war is over, and though the shortages continue, I find time to work on the house. I scrub the floorboards in my bedroom and paint them a rich golden brown, the color of honey. I dye new curtains and a cover for my bed. I paint the walls and ceiling and door. My waters break at five o'clock on Christmas Eve. Bunny cycles for the doctor while Duncan helps me to my room. It is an easy birth. I steady myself against the mantel of the fireplace between contractions. I ask to hold the baby immediately she is born. The doctor nods his consent. The midwife wraps her in a clean towel and hands her to me. Her fingers flex in tiny star shapes. I cradle my new daughter tight against my breast then set her in her father's arms.

Later that day we exchange our presents. Bunny peers at the baby, exclaiming with delight when she opens her eyes. He quips that as soon as she is old enough he will marry her. As he reaches into the crib to lift her, I am seized with a fear that he will steal her too.

I am working on a woodcut. My daughter sleeps in her crib by my side. I look at her every few minutes, marveling at her beauty. I am carving my picture of the bathtub. This time, I place my figure directly in front of it. The woman's eyes remain lowered to the floor; her hands are still fastening her plait, but now her body curves into the ample roundness of the bath. There are just two flowers in the vase in the arched window. Though they bend in opposite directions, they are in perfect symmetry. I try out names for my daughter while I work: Clarissa, Rachel, Helen. I cannot think of one good enough for her. She is a heaven-sent angel, the answer to a prayer. I fashion her future as I cut into the wood. She will be a great artist. She will succeed where I have failed. I sculpt my figure's haunches until they are as voluptuous as the maternal contours of the bath.

8

"THANK YOU FOR COMING."

I follow Leonard into the sitting room, where we install ourselves on either side of the fireplace.

"How long has she been unwell?" I find it hard to hide my annoyance; it would have been so much easier to care for Angelica if I had been able to leave Julian and Quentin with you as we had arranged. Leonard sighs.

"She's been having headaches for some time, but it's this recent bout of flu that has laid her low. I felt I had to ask you to collect the boys."

"I see. Are they in the garden?"

"Yes."

I get up and walk to the window, hoping to catch a glimpse of Julian and Quentin at play. On the table in front of the window are several pieces of paper covered in your writing, surrounded by bottles of ink and pens. As I stoop to look more closely, I realize that the pages are decorated with the children's sketches. I pick up one of the sheets.

"These are lovely," I say, studying the drawings.

"Yes," Leonard acknowledges, "it was one of Virginia's ideas for keeping the boys occupied while they were here. Her original plan was to produce a play, but I persuaded her it would be more restful if they worked on something where she could sit down. I know she's sorry not to be able to finish the story with them.'"

I examine a cartoon figure of a woman in a large hat pedaling furiously on a bicycle.

"Is she really so ill?"

"Dr. Fergusson is worried about her heart. He wants her to see a specialist in Wimpole Street."

I gaze at Leonard.

"So you think it might be her heart this time rather than her old problem?"

"I'm not sure it's possible to separate them. Whatever it is, she's taken it seriously enough to agree that she shouldn't have the boys."

"Can I see her?"

Leonard nods his consent and I make my way to your room. You are not in bed as I had expected but sitting upright in a chair, your writing board on your knee. You look up as I come in.

"I thought I heard a car."

I sit down on the bed.

"How is Angelica?" you ask, arranging your pages in a pile.

"To be absolutely honest I'm not sure." I stare at the floor, wondering how the nurse is coping.

"Nessa . . ." You hold out your hand. "I'm sorry. I've let you down. You know how much I was looking forward to having the boys here."

"Were you?" I cannot prevent the shrill note of accusation.

"Of course. I'd made all sorts of plans for things to do with them. Leonard insisted on calling you."

"And you do everything Leonard says?"

You let your outstretched hand drop to your lap.

"I owe him so much, Ness. You can't imagine all he does for me."

I look away. I remember the anxious concern in Leonard's voice as we spoke on the telephone, the expression of tenderness that came over his face as we talked about you in the sitting room.

"I'd be lost without him. I just wish that sometimes . . . he'd let me flex my wings a little."

I think of Duncan's affair with Bunny, his prolonged absences from home.

"And what would you do if you could flex your wings?"

"Oh, lots of things. Have children, for instance."

"It's not too late."

You look at me in scorn.

"Of course it is! I'm forty."

"And I'm forty-two."

"It's always been easier for you."

I stand up. I am tired of these old arguments.

"I must go and gather up the boys." I turn toward the door.

"Dearest . . ." I hesitate. I hear the plaintive tone in your voice. "You know this isn't how I wanted my life to be." I stare at you in your chair, huddled in your blanket, your writing on your knee.

"I love the story you are working on with the children."

"Do you?" Your face lights up. "Perhaps you'll let the boys come and stay once I'm better."

☙

We sit in the garden of your new home, our deck chairs facing each other. The apple trees are in blossom and the breeze scatters pink and white petals at our feet.

"Of course," you say, pouring out the tea, "it was a blow finally having to give up Asheham."

From the corner of my eye, I watch Julian and Quentin help Leonard remove a dead branch from one of the trees. The sound of sawing punctuates our talk.

"Still," you go on, as you hand me a cup, "it's a comfort to know that we own this house. No one can dislodge us from here."

The dead branch splinters then plummets to the ground. The boys descend on it with jubilant cheers.

"I was wondering whether you would come and do some decorating for us."

I look up. I had not expected this. I do not know whether to be pleased or insulted. I could certainly use the money. To buy myself time, I ask about your work.

"Will it be a good place to write in, do you think?"

"I hope so. Actually, I've begun a new novel. Leonard calls it my ghost story."

I shift my position. I watch Leonard and Julian drag the dead branch to the woodshed, leaving a frail mosaic of blossom in their wake. Soon the petals will seep through the mesh of grass and rot in the damp earth.

"And who is the ghost?"

Your reply is so faint that at first I do not hear you.

"Thoby."

I start.

"You're writing a novel about Thoby?"

"Yes. I didn't intend to. I began with the idea that you can never get inside another person's life — not really — and the life that came into focus as I wrote was Thoby's."

I consider your answer. I remember the letters you wrote to Violet after Thoby died, spinning out the fiction that he was still alive. You hesitate.

"I thought you would be pleased."

I set a canvas on my easel. I pick up my brush. I paint falteringly, badly. I force myself to apply one stroke after another, building up my shapes. I do it because I do not know what else to do. I am certain the result will be a failure. I paint the doorway and the open door. I paint a chair and a table on the near side of the door and, directly opposite it, another chair, set against the shrubbery. The door itself I leave in shadow. It is of no interest and too small to fill the space. I come back to my chairs. I work a blue cushion, edged in scarlet, on the garden chair. The brightness emphasizes its vacancy. It is an absurd chair, wedged between the open door and the garden. It looks in instead of out. I make the chair inside the door more elegant. I give it a rounded back, carved legs. I cannot decide on the shade. I try gray, brown, blue. None are right but I do not mind. I determine to leave the color unresolved. I work a darker square on the seat. This time it is a notebook instead of a cushion, the pages clearly visible between the covers. Down the sides of the picture I paint a pair of dark curtains, framing the chairs. I want to highlight their redundancy, draw attention to their feud.

I open the package, surprised to see it addressed in Leonard's hand. I pull out the pages that are inside and spread them on the table. I see at once that Leonard has altered the setting of my woodcuts. All the instructions I wrote so painstakingly have been ignored. I shake with rage. I will not have my illustrations ruined by Leonard's poor judgment! I cannot believe you have allowed him to ride roughshod over my designs. I write to you, saying what I think of your arrogance and amateurism. I tell you I never want to work with you or Leonard again.

It is too cold to paint outside so we have taken our easels upstairs, where we can look out across the pond. The bare branches of the willows cast strange reflections on the glassy surface, like witches' hair. I choose a corner of the garden as my subject, two trees, a segment of wall, the fields and sky beyond. Duncan has set his easel slightly ahead of mine. As I work, I can see the slope of his head and shoulders, the movement of his hand. I find it hard to convey the modulations of the light. I work crimson into the bark of the trees, a ribbon of coral in the grain of the wall. The light shifts again. I add silver and cerulean to the sky. Duncan stops painting and sits down on the bed.

"He'll marry. I do know that."

I realize he is talking about Bunny.

"Yes, I suppose he will."

"Mallory has married. Adrian has married. Even Maynard thinks of marrying. They'll all succumb."

"Except you?" It is the question I hardly dare ask.

"Except me."

I look up and see the hopeless expression on Duncan's face.

"Nessa. I wish I could."

My hand trembles. I sense Duncan watching me, gauging

my reaction. I look at the trees I have painted, the wall, the sky. Perhaps, if I stare at the shapes hard enough, I will find a reason to go on.

"Ness."

He wants me to absolve him, to tell him it makes no difference. I gaze out the window and notice a clump of young shoots nestling in the shelter of the wall. I turn back to my canvas.

"Let's finish our pictures."

We are in the sitting room at Charleston. We have been listening to Maynard's account of the peace settlement, and this has led to a discussion about the wisdom of laying down one's life for the general cause. Roger, who has been rebuilding the fire, sits back on his heels.

"Do you really think people, when they enlist, ask themselves the question? I'm thinking of the men I've known. They talk about the fighting and the hardship, but not about dying. Not overtly, anyway."

Maynard leans forward.

"The thought must be there, though. Especially as time goes on and the numbers of dead increase."

Roger does not reply. He folds sheets of newspaper into neat concertinas and tucks them between the logs.

"I can imagine agreeing to give up my life, as long as I could be sure that the world would be a better place as a consequence." Duncan's voice seems to float from his perch by the window.

"Ah! There's the rub! Who could promise that? And then you have to ask yourself how long the benefit would endure. Would it last your anticipated lifetime — in which case I suppose the sum would balance itself and it would be worth the price — or would it peter out after only a few years?" There is no mistaking the cynicism in Maynard's tone.

"Well I for one could never be persuaded that my life would be worth the sacrifice! I'd tussle Picasso for the last seat on the boat — and I certainly wouldn't hesitate if all that was at stake was a strip of land!" We all laugh at Clive's ebullience. Roger sets a match to his paper and wood edifice and looks at me.

"What does Woman say? Are we merely revealing the limitations of our sex?"

I watch the flames catch, greedy tongues gobbling the paper.

"I can imagine being prepared to die — for an artist I believed in, for instance."

I feel Roger's eyes burrow into me. I know what he is thinking. I read his unspoken plea to let Duncan go.

Bunny's defection changes nothing, except that now Duncan pursues his love affairs away from home. My life while Duncan is gone revolves around the post. In the mornings, the leap of hope as I watch the postman carry his bag up the drive. Racing to the hall to scrutinize the pile of envelopes, praying that today there will be one in Duncan's hand. Ripping the letter open and skimming it quickly to see if the general purport is good or bad. Reading the lines more slowly, poring over them until I have learned them by heart. Carrying them round with me, while I work in the garden, as I paint, trying to penetrate any hidden signals. The words twisting and gibing in my mind until I no longer know whether "I hope you are happy" means "I am blissfully in love and do not need you" or whether it means "I miss you and will come home to you soon." The joy and ordeal of replying. I sit at the table and get out my paper

144

and pen. I smooth the paper flat, letting the movement still my mind. I never write until I am calm. Only then do I trust myself to set down words that will not frighten, will not beg. I make my phrases as neutral as I can. News of the house, Angelica, mutual friends, all the things we share. I dare not express the thoughts that wash round my head, admit my loneliness and yearning. Instead I talk about the roses, a new mural in the hall. I offer the lures of home, whatever temptations I can conjure to persuade Duncan to return.

There is the day a letter comes full of foreboding. A doctor has diagnosed typhoid. I have scarcely finished reading before I am flying round the house, throwing clothes and wash things into bags. All I can think of as I grasp Angelica by the hand and hurry to the station is that I must get to Duncan as quickly as I can. Images of Thoby beat in my head. As we take our seats in the train, I see reflections of Thoby's coffin in the grimy carriage windows. Angelica huddles close to her nurse, frightened of the mother I have become. We cross the channel, make our way to Paris, yet even here I dare not stop. I force us on, weary and dazed, terrified in case I arrive too late.

We take a cab from the station. As we drive along the narrow lanes my one preoccupation is to reach Duncan's side. We pull up at the house and I jump out and ring the bell. A maid shows us into a sitting room. I gaze at neatly clipped box hedges through the open window. Eventually an elegantly dressed woman appears. I recognize her at once as Duncan's mother. She shakes my hand, thanks me for my concern. She assures me that Duncan is recovering. I see her take in our bedraggled clothes, the chaos of our luggage. Her eyes stray to Angelica and her mouth sets in a firm line. When I ask if I can see Duncan she shakes her head, confident of her prerogative.

She asks me where we are staying and her smile hardly falters as I tell her we have only just arrived. She bids us goodbye on the pretext of our being tired, adding over her shoulder that we must call again once Duncan is well. She leaves the maid to show us to the door. Our cab has long since departed and we have no alternative but to walk back to town.

I have no status. I am neither wife nor lover, not family or friend. I sit in the hotel bedroom and stare out to sea. If I lean out the window far enough I can glimpse the house where Duncan is convalescing. When I am finally allowed to see him I realize it is not only his mother who is against me. My coming has made him a laughingstock. He scarcely addresses a word to me.

I rent a villa. I cannot afford to continue paying for hotel rooms and I have no choice but to remain. Duncan visits Angelica, and he and I paint in the garden, savoring the bold Mediterranean colors, the great glancing planes of light. Gradually his anger toward me abates. When his mother returns to England he moves in with me.

You visit, with Leonard. We walk down to the harbor, enjoying the corridor of cool between the narrow rows of houses. You loop your arm through mine, and as we come out onto the quay we stop and watch the fishermen unloading their catch. You tell me how envious you are of the companionable way Duncan and I paint together, compared to your solitariness as a writer. We are like brother and sister, you say, fond yet inviolably chaste. With the surety of lightning, you scissor my sky into halves. I stare at a group of alluringly dressed young women gossiping and laughing as they wait for their men at the end of the quay. Your words leave me as shriveled and exposed as the starfish strung up to dry and sold for a few centimes to passersby.

I have a recurring dream. In it I am sitting by a window, looking out over a garden. I am wearing Mother's green shawl and there is a boy by my side. He is cutting shapes from a magazine, frowning as he concentrates on his task. You are in the garden, reclining in a deck chair, your notebook open on your knee. I watch your hand move implacably across your page. Suddenly I become aware of a presence in the doorway. I look up and glimpse a man's outline, but the brilliance of the light prevents me from making out his features. I suspect it is Duncan though I cannot be sure. He comes over to me and lays his hand on my shoulder. I feel the child stir beside me, restive and jealous. I sense that I am needed, though part of me longs to go on sitting quietly by the window, my child by my side. I rouse myself and turn to the man. To my astonishment he has disappeared. I glance toward the door but all I can see is the vacant frame and the light. I look back at the garden. Your chair is empty. The only sign that you have been sitting there is the notebook you have laid face down on the grass. I turn to the child but he, too, has vanished, leaving a trail of paper cutouts on the floor. I stare at the absence.

I reread the first paragraph of Duncan's letter again. I feel a fresh stab of pain each time I come across the new name. I gaze at the daisies that have seeded themselves in the lawn. A gust of fear rips through me. What if this time the affair lasts and Duncan does not return? I force myself to my feet and head out through the gate. I walk until the dark presses round me.

Julian is asleep in a chair when I go in. His head rests against his hand and I feel a rush of tenderness as I bend over and kiss his cheek. He opens his eyes and stares at me with an expression of such loathing that for a moment I am taken aback. I stoop to kiss him again but he pushes me away. He jumps from his chair and runs past me. I follow him to his room but he refuses to speak to me. It is only the next day that I realize I walked out on his birthday.

This dream is different. I am lying on my front, tracing the pattern in the carpet with my fingers. I mark the intricate twist of stem and leaves, the great loops of flowers. Above me is the familiar roof of the nursery table. If I turn my head, I spy the skirted legs of the maids. Their chatter as they sort the laundry is a soothing accompaniment to my play. There is a warm feeling along my flank and if I turn my head the other way I see Thoby. His body is so close to mine as to be almost indistinguishable from it. I sense that I must keep still and quiet or this warmth will go away. While I am thinking this, something shifts. I lose my place in the maze of leaves and flowers. I realize Thoby has gone. The space where his body was is empty and cold. Though I cry out no one hears me. The maids seem oblivious of what has happened. I look down but the shapes and colors have all disappeared. There is nothing left. I decide to fill the blankness by creating my own patterns. No matter how hard I work, I cannot replace what I have lost.

It is Sunday and I am alone; I have sent the children to stay with Clive. For once there are no visitors. I am in the sitting room at Charleston, where I have been waiting since early morning, wondering why Duncan does not come. Ever since his letter arrived announcing his return I have thought of little

else. I have cleaned and decorated every room, trying to anticipate his needs. Now that his affair is over, I can admit that ending it will have been painful. He will need space to recover I
remind myself. I resolve to force nothing on him, ask nothing for myself. To have him with me again will be recompense
enough.

I watch the light spill through the curtains onto the floor.
For the thousandth time, I try not to wonder why Duncan did
not come at the time he stated in his letter. I know the line by
heart. *I will be with you for dinner.* The places are still laid in
the dining room, the duck congealing on its plate on the sideboard. I sat at the table and watched the candles burn themselves out, starting to my feet with each spatter of rain on the
gravel, every gust of wind in the trees. Eventually, as dawn
broke, I rose and came in here.

It is well into the afternoon before I hear Duncan's voice. I
force myself to swallow the great rush of emotion that immediately floods every nerve. The marigolds I have arranged on the
table throb with light. I cannot prevent the surge of hope that
this time he comes to stay.

Duncan appears in the doorway. Something in his demeanor
makes me freeze. He sidles past me with only a perfunctory pat
on my shoulder and flops into a chair. All the weeks of waiting,
all my pent-up loneliness, well up inside me.

"I was expecting you last night."

Duncan groans and sinks further into his chair.

"I was worried. I didn't know what had happened." I school
myself to wait for Duncan's reply.

"Nessa. I'm here now."

My anger is churning and spilling and I cannot keep it in.

"I suppose you think this is all my life is? Waiting for you."

149

Duncan's eyes narrow. I see him stare at the painted angel on the wood box. We worked on it together, laughing as we argued over the position of the wings. For one terrifying moment I realize Duncan might leave for good. Immediately, I am on the defensive. I rein in my feelings.

"I'm sorry. You must be tired after your journey. I'll make some tea."

The vexed expression on Duncan's face accompanies me to the kitchen.

It is dark, save for the slivers of moonlight that slip out from behind the crack in the curtains. I lie with my cheek on the pillow, listening. My body is taut with longing. I close my eyes and imagine I hear her tread on the stairs. I do not doubt she will come. I think of the cool of her arms as she stoops to kiss me, the feel of her gloved fingers as she sweeps the loose strands of hair back behind my ears. I open my eyes and watch the pale light quiver in the draft. I strain to hear her footsteps but the only sound is the cadence of your breathing on the other side of the room. Still I do not doubt she will come. I try to remember what dress Mother is wearing. I picture the blue velvet, the folds of her skirt falling round her like the sea. I think of all the guests she must say goodnight to, the scurry in the hall to find hats and coats and umbrellas. I imagine the horses' hooves slipping on the wet cobbles, the drowsy, lulling, rocking warmth inside the cabs.

My eyes open with a start. I sit up and lift the edge of the curtains. There are streaks of gray in the sky. I can see the branches of the trees, rain dripping from their leaves. My disappointment streams in torrents down the pane.

∽

The gramophone sends its tune strutting and cavalcading about the room. Several couples are already dancing. I am struck by the lavishness of your new London residence. The chairs have been re-covered in a bold yellow check, there are green glass ornaments on the mantelshelf, new lamps. You are talking to a woman I do not recognize. I study the crop of dark, shingled hair swept back off the forehead, the deep-set eyes, the lascivious mouth. I remember your last letter, in which you mentioned meeting a daughter of the Sackville family, the novelist Vita Sackville-West. Splendid, was how you described her: aristocratic, arrogant, and dressed like a parakeet. You could not abide her society small talk and did not think you would see her again. The music jigs and frisks. I watch you catch hold of Vita, and playfully, commandingly, lead her to the middle of the floor. All eyes are upon you. Vita is dressed in flamboyant orange silk trousers, two black feathers in her hair. You dip and hop and slide to one of the new dance steps. As you spin Vita round, you fling your arms above your head, wild and free. The tune slows and you let your cheek rest on Vita's breast, your hips gyrating as you two-step back and forth. Everyone claps as the dance ends. You survey your audience and take a deep bow, your face flushed and ecstatic. You lead Vita to the side of the room where refreshments have been set out on a table. You whisper something in her ear as you hand her a drink, and the two of you roar with laughter. I look round for Duncan. He is standing by the window, talking to Tom. I wonder when it will be decent for me to leave.

You come toward me. You find an empty chair and set it beside mine, your eyes still shining from the triumph of your dance. The gramophone sends out a new tune. Lydia pulls a reluctant Maynard to his feet.

"So," you begin, "what do you think of her?"

I gaze at Vita. She is smoking a cigarette and takes a deep draft as she scans the assembled company. I feel her eyes rest on me.

"She considers me as I imagine an Arab horse might consider a long-eared donkey."

You laugh, pleased with the wit of my reply.

"She certainly has a pedigree. Did I tell you her ancestors go back to the Norman Conquest?"

I say nothing. A young man has approached Vita and I watch them fall into conversation.

"I'm thinking of copying her and getting my hair shingled."

I start with surprise. You wink at me.

"Why not? It's time we moved on. Besides, imagine not having to rely on hairpins!"

I push a stray wisp of my own hair back into place and stare at you. Your dark satin and lace come into focus.

"Is that why you're wearing Mother's dress?"

You ignore my needling and lean close.

"Be honest: don't you think she's magnificent?"

"Since you do everything to stir up my jealousy I shall refuse to answer."

"I do no such thing!" You let your voice drop in tone. "We've asked her to write a book for the press." I see the gleam of mischief in your eye. "It should do extremely well. She's very much in demand as an author. I wouldn't be surprised if she wins a prize."

I shift uncomfortably in my chair. I wish Duncan would come and find me.

"Actually, I'm thinking of writing a book about her. After all, you always complain if I write about you." You look at me archly. "I thought I might try something different. Something playful and light. A spoof historical drama, for instance. We could do with new forms for all the old feelings, don't you think? How about Vita as an Elizabethan courtier? I see her mustached and manly — though there again, she'd make a splendidly exotic foreign princess."

There is a picture I should like to paint. I see it sometimes in my mind's eye, when I lie awake at night unable to sleep, or in the early morning as the light circles the walls, before the rest of the house stirs. Sometimes it stares back at me as I gaze into the fire, or I catch glimpses of it lodged in the trees as I walk through the garden. In the painting we are seated on opposite sides of a table. Next to me is a child in a highchair — Thoby, perhaps. Next to you is a figure I always assume must be Father. Mother presides. Though she has her back to us her profile is clearly visible. The reason I do not try to paint this portrait is that it is never still. While it always contains the same elements — you, me, the child in the highchair, the two adults — they constantly rearrange themselves. Sometimes the alterations are so great that one of the figures disappears altogether. This happens most particularly with Mother, perhaps because of her prominence in the design. Whenever she is absent I take her place. It is as if there is a mysterious force at work, so that whenever the shape that designates Mother vanishes, my own form changes to fill the space. I can do nothing to prevent this movement. I know in some obscure part of myself that if I try to block it the space will engulf the entire picture. I realize that my function in the painting is to stop this from happening. I am simultaneously inside the portrait, a mark on the canvas, and outside it, the artist. Sometimes you are an ally in the picture, sometimes a child that requires protection; sometimes your proximity is a threat. Whenever your opposition becomes too powerful I have no choice but to deploy all the weapons at my disposal to force your retreat. Yet I cannot risk losing you altogether. While other parts of the painting emerge and recede without disaster, you are necessary to its equilibrium.

I tell no one of this nightmare haunting. I do what I can to keep it at bay. I decorate round it with figures and flowers, landscapes, abstract patterns. Occasionally, as I contemplate the images, I suspect that the void may not be so terrifying, and I am tempted to examine it more closely. Yet something holds me back. I fear that the impression is an illusion, a chimera designed to lure me into oblivion, which I must resist at all costs.

Once, just once, I attempt to paint Mother facing outward. I gather all the photographs I have of her and stand them in a row. The one I like best is the one in which she is wearing a lace cap. She is still a young woman in the picture, though there is an expression of suffering in her eyes that reveals her depth of experience. As I stare at the photograph I realize that by the time it was taken she had already lost her first husband, a man she loved. This is what you see in her face, that inner knowledge of loss. Her features are exquisite. I study the arched cheekbones, the finely wrought nose. Her skin is so smooth it could be alabaster. A frieze of overhanging leaves surrounds her so that she appears to be emerging from a wood. She might be a character in a myth. My painting beckons. I cannot work with Mother watching me. I take her photographs down.

I start, then stop, then obliterate what I have done. I create a backdrop of greenery, the path and summerhouse in the

154

garden, a table with a vase of flowers. The pinks and lilacs of my peonies and foxgloves wrangle with my crimson poppies. All the while the central space looms. Every time I try to paint Mother's face or the outline of her body as she rests in her chair, the shapes miscarry, the structure collapses. It is as if I dare not alter the design. You could. You succeeded where I failed. You were not embroiled as I was. The portrait of Mother you drew in your novel was so convincing that I heard her voice, saw the perpendicular of her back, as I read. I gaze at my picture. The emptiness remains. I paint a random figure, hurriedly, haphazardly, to fill the space, then take the canvas down. It is only years later when I look at the picture again that I realize the figure is my daughter.

The trees at this time of year look like broken fans, their bare branches splaying in all directions. We are sitting on the terrace in Cassis, where I have kept on the villa I rented for the summer. It is mild despite the lateness of the season. You are reading, pen in hand. Every now and then you pause to write a thought in your notebook. You look absorbed, settled, as if you are engaging with your author — it is Proust, I think — as an equal. I open the newspaper and leaf through the pages, stopping at the pictures. Compared to you I am an intellectual butterfly.

"What do you think about this business of Adrian's?" I ask at length.

You look up.

"What do you mean?"

"This psychoanalysis he has embarked on."

You lay your book face down on your knee.

"It's ludicrous! Like everything else Adrian takes up. Have

155

you seen him recently? He's developed this irritating habit of nodding knowingly at everything you say — as if he sees a hidden message behind it. I find it infuriating."

"Do you think it will help him?"

You snort.

"Only because it gives him someone to blame! You do realize it's all our fault. We ignored him when we were children and this led him to repress his feelings."

"That's absurd!" I remember Adrian as a child and sigh. "I suppose we could have done more for him."

You cast me a withering glance.

"Don't you start. I've heard more than enough about thwarted desires from Lytton. Why is everyone suddenly talking about Freud? I don't even want to think how his theories apply to Adrian."

I giggle.

"Perhaps it's because you threw your breakfast eggs at him."

"Of course! All that dribbling yellow yolk and sullied white! His psychoanalyst must be having a field day."

We both roar with laughter. You make a few more caustic comments about Adrian, then return to your book. I find a pencil and sketch a pot of late-flowering geraniums on the terrace. The drawing is not a success. I misjudge the angle, fail to catch the play of light. To my relief, Elise brings out the letters. I sort through the envelopes, seizing on one with a Cambridge postmark.

"It's from Julian," I announce, loudly, ostentatiously, tearing it open. I gulp down Julian's account of a supper party, a new tutor, a boating expedition on the Cam. His words revive me. Your reading of Proust, all your books, recede to their proper size.

"He's doing very well. His tutor has said some encouraging things about his essays. He predicts a first."

I prattle without thinking. You look at the letter lying open on my knee.

"Let me see."

I know as soon as I have handed it to you that it is a mistake. The letter has caught you off-guard. You have always been jealous of Julian. I watch you read with a sinking heart.

"He mentions the copy of *Orlando* I sent him." Your voice is casual, light. "I wish he would say how he likes it. Did I tell you Leonard estimates we have made £2,000 already from its sales?"

Your barb hits home. I feel it ripping through muscle and sinew. You know perfectly well that I make almost nothing from my painting, that I can scarcely afford to pay my models. You finish Julian's letter and give it back to me. I hide it in my pocket.

9

THE FRAME OF A WINDOW, BLUE PAINT BLISTERING
in the Mediterranean sun. I am arrested, dazzled by color, the
cascading scarlet of a pot of hibiscus, the glaring whitewash of
a wall. It is as if the colors, first separately, then collectively,
strike a series of notes that sets up a resonating chord in me. I
am impelled to paint it. I am forced to convey the impact of
the red against the blue, the white against the red. Perhaps this
compulsion is a flaw. When I paint, I think only of what is before me.

Turn and turn again. I peer into the kaleidoscope of memory and see the patterns shift and fall, first in a star formation,
then in an oblong as the points broaden out and touch. The
truth has many sides to it, many changing shapes and forms. I
was distraught as my work became increasingly marginalized
in comparison with yours, but I also reveled in my obscurity.

You smooth the rectangle of paper flat on the table and take
a good pinch of tobacco from the tin. You arrange the fibers

in a column, then roll one of the sides of the paper inward to keep the tobacco in place. You lick the remaining edge, furl it round the center, and press it into shape. Finally you lift the cigarette to your mouth and light it from one of the candles. You sit back and take a deep draft.

Quentin, with whom you have been arguing about the General Strike, snorts.

"So this is your answer, is it? Indulging yourself on a terrace a thousand miles from the coalface!" He holds up the jug of red wine. His tone is teasing, jocular. You push your empty glass toward him, grinning.

"Of course we all saw how it would end. The TUC selling the miners short, then being diddled in their turn."

Leonard groans.

"It was the usual human story. The side with the most right on it becoming political capital for the prejudices and aspirations of all the others — and getting crushed in the process."

There is silence as Leonard's seriousness introduces an unwelcome tone in what has been an exceptionally merry evening. You snigger.

"Do you remember Baldwin? His absurd speech on the radio. He bellowed away as if he were standing on Speakers' Corner. Listening with Pinker on my knee, I couldn't stop thinking how pompous he sounded. This is the Prime Minister, I kept telling myself, so why don't I feel more respect?"

Leonard, smiling now, reaches for your hand. You kiss him.

"How we argued about it! You were all disillusionment and action, while I . . ."

"Saved everything up and used it in some sketch!"

"What's the good of pessimism?" You wink at Quentin. "Especially in a place like this."

You gesture toward the bay, your cigarette a tiny dot of light against the dark. I gaze at the view. The hillside is cloaked in blackness, the sky studded with stars. In the distance, discernible only by its sound, is the brooding presence of the sea. The air is warm for the time of year and full of the scent of wild thyme. I look round at the assembled company. We have eaten and laughed and told wild stories. Tomorrow I will paint while Angelica has her French lesson, then Duncan will drive us to the beach. I feel content and surrounded by the good things in life. You catch my mood.

"It's perfect, isn't it! If we were in England now we'd still be huddled up in our separate houses, crouching over lonely fires. None of this sitting out in company under the dreaming expanse of the night sky." You look at Leonard. "Shall we confess our sin?"

You glance round the table to make sure all eyes are on you.

"Today," you begin with great importance, "Leonard and I went to look at the villa."

I start. This is not what I had expected you to say.

"But I thought it was too expensive."

You raise your eyebrows.

"Ah, but not if you are a consummate negotiator."

I am staring at you now, wondering what you mean.

"I simply told the man, did I not Leonard, that the villa was too expensive, but that we would consider renting it from him."

"And did he agree?" I ask quickly.

"Of course. We are to put in new windows and bring our own furniture — and the villa is ours whenever we want it for 300 francs a month."

"But that's nothing!"

You beam at me.

"You see! I wasn't exaggerating."

"Does this mean the villa will no longer be up for sale?" I lean forward to hear your answer to Duncan's question. You take another draft of your cigarette.

"We didn't get a final agreement on that," you concede.

"Well, then." I can feel the relief flooding back. "It's hardly a bargain if you pay for new windows and the villa is immediately sold to someone else!"

You refuse to be swerved and raise your glass.

"But it won't be sold! So here's a toast to our new life in Cassis."

You flash me one of your most beguiling smiles.

Later, as I am on my way to my room, you stop me. You lead me into the sitting room and settle down on the sofa.

"I need to talk to you. I don't understand your reaction to the villa. After all, you spent most of last summer trying to persuade us to move here!"

I sit beside you and try to still my racing mind. What you say is true. I thought that if I could persuade you to take a house here I would not need to return to England for the winter. Yet the idea that you might be living directly opposite suddenly feels alarming.

"I'm worried that you wouldn't be happy, that's all." I stumble over my words. "Our lives are so different here — we live very simply."

"Exactly!" Your eyes are shining now.

I force myself to go on.

"I'm not sure it would suit you."

"Nonsense." You wave your arm, as if to shoo away an unwelcome fly. "Leonard and I have become far too embroiled in England. It would do us the world of good to get away."

"It's just that . . . the things that matter to me — painting, the children — this is the perfect place for them."

The wine I have drunk at dinner is pulsing through my veins, making me say things I know I will regret. I press on regardless.

"What I mean is . . . your life is very different. You need libraries, people — it doesn't matter where I am as long as . . ."

"As long as I'm near you." The pleading in your voice makes it hard for me to rebut you. You edge closer.

"Nessa . . . I honestly don't think I can stand it if you move here for good. My life in England feels barren — dry — with you gone. You make the world dance."

To stop my head from reeling, I rest it against your chest.

"Don't be silly," I venture, my words half-muffled by your dress, "you'll manage perfectly well without me! After all," I add, lifting my head, "with me gone, you can do what you like best." I plant a kiss on your cheek.

"And what might that be?" you ask.

"Why — you can invent me to your heart's content."

Angelica sees it first, pointing excitedly as it flies in through the open window. We fall silent as it circles the room before settling on the lamp in the center of the table. I have never seen such a large specimen.

"Is it a bat?" Angelica wonders in an awed whisper.

Duncan shakes his head.

"It's a moth," he tells her, "an emperor, I should guess, from its size."

"Why does it keep going round and round the lamp?" Angelica's whisper is louder now.

"It's attracted to the light," you inform her. "It thinks it can get inside."

I gaze at the moth for a moment, then stand up and close the window. Angelica hisses at me.

"Don't do that. It won't be able to get out."

I ignore her disgruntled frown.

"Can you get your butterfly net from the hall? Let's try and catch it for Julian's collection."

Angelica runs obediently into the hall and returns with her net. I take it from her. The moth continues its slow worshiping spiral round the lamp. I gauge my stroke, yet even I am surprised by the creature's fierce resistance. I keep the net pressed against the glass and after some minutes the moth ceases to struggle. Angelica has gone pale.

"Oh Mummy, let it go. It's too big. Don't kill it."

I pick up a magazine and slide it across the open end of the net. I set the net on the table and weight the handle with a book. Then I go into the kitchen and return with a jar of chloroform and a rag. Angelica is crying now, tugging at my sleeve as I remove the stopper from the jar and pour some of the chloroform onto the rag. I look at the moth trapped inside the net. Its wings are covered in fur, pale tawny brown. I imagine the lash of release if I were to lift the net and set the creature free.

"It will die soon anyway." Leonard's words seem decisive. Angelica stares at him, then at me. You nod. I raise the net an inch and put the chloroform-soaked rag inside. For a moment no one speaks.

"Come on," I say to Angelica at last, holding out my hand, "time for bed."

That night, as I lie awake, I seem to hear the soft flutter of wings circle the ceiling above my head. I think about Angelica's plea for mercy, Leonard's commonsense remark, my determination to capture the moth for Julian. I remember Stella, Thoby, Mother. How preposterous their dying seemed.

I get out of bed and throw a shawl round my shoulders. The sitting room is dark except for a shaft of moonlight from the uncurtained window. The net is still on the table, held in place by the book. I go over to it and peer in. I can see the moth clearly in the moonlight. It seems smaller now that it is at rest. I open the window and feel the cool air flood the room. I pick up the net with the magazine still pressing against it and take it over to the window. Then I lift the magazine and shake the moth gently free. I remain for some time watching in vain for the moth's flight. Finally I close the window.

As I turn to go I see your silhouette in the doorway.

"I thought I heard you come in here. Is it dead?"

"I think so. I tried to let it go though I didn't see it fly away."

"You goose. So now you've offended everyone. You can't tell Angelica it's alive and nor can you give Julian his prize."

"It's true Julian would have loved it."

You come over to the window.

"What wouldn't you do for those brats of yours! I sometimes think you'd boil me in oil if it afforded them pleasure."

I laugh despite myself.

"Would you like some cocoa?"

We go into the kitchen and I turn on the light. You sit down at the table while I put a pan of milk to heat on the stove.

"Do you remember the moth tree?" you ask suddenly.

I put a spoon of cocoa into two mugs and look up.

"You know — the one Father painted with treacle in St. Ives so that we could catch moths. I always had mixed feelings about it."

"I remember Father's collection. Everything in strict alphabetical order with the name written out underneath."

I pour the milk into the mugs and sit down opposite you at the table.

"I used to think that was what adult life was like. Everything organized and in its place." I gaze round the kitchen. There are dirty dishes in the sink, a mound of clothes waiting to be washed by the tub. I sigh.

"My adult life has turned out exactly the opposite." I gather up some unfinished drawings on the table and put them to one side. "Bits and pieces, like the scraps of sewing at the bottom of Mother's work basket. Nothing finished, nothing made good."

You stare at me.

"At least you have all the strands. They're in your hands."

"By that reckoning every adult life's a success!"

You shrug.

"No, Ness. You hold the light. Then there are lonely moths like me circling the lamp, searching for a way in."

"I knew you'd make a scene out of it! So what about all the other people sitting round the table tonight? How do they feature in your sketch?"

You lean back and gaze at me steadily.

"They personify the different voices — emblematized by the moth."

"Sounds like the start for one of your novels."

✎

I read down the guest list and wonder, too late, if it was wise to invite so many people. To quell my fears I pace up and down, surveying the furniture Duncan and I have painted. Scarcely an object has been left untouched: there are murals on the walls, and even the piano in the center of the room has been decorated. At one end there is a display of the items we hope to sell.

Roger is the first to arrive.

"It's a triumph! You will be feted and adored across London!"

I smile at his flattery. He has scarcely even glanced at our things. Before I can tease him, other guests appear. I station myself behind the drinks table and hand out glasses of punch. I try not to hear what is being said about our work.

I spy Lytton in a corner of the room and wave to him. He comes across at once.

"My dear, I didn't realize you had attracted the gentlemen of the press in quite such droves! I'm positively exhausted having to explain the difference between Provençal and Italianate. I hate to think how they will mangle it!"

We become aware of a commotion near the door. I see you enter, followed by a stout, gray-haired woman in a shabby suit and tricornered hat. News of your arrival shoots through the room like an electric spark. Lytton adjusts his monocle to get a better view.

"Ah, the divine Virginia, causing her habitual stir! How delightful that she should be here. Our paths hardly ever seem to cross these days."

"She's one of the patrons of the show. She's pledged to spend at least £100 — and says she doesn't much mind what she has."

Lytton laughs.

"Our friends from the newspapers flock round her like the vultures they are, hoping, no doubt, for some appetizing morsels about the new book. Still, with you as my *carte d'entrée*, we should be able to cut through."

Lytton sets off boldly in your direction. I trail reluctantly behind. I would have liked to ask about Carrington. The crowd congregating round you increases in size. I should have known that even at my show you would steal the limelight. A loud, bellicose voice fanfares above the hubbub.

"My dear man, since when have the press ever got anything right?"

I strain to catch a glimpse of what is happening. The voice battles on.

"I have told you, Mrs. Woolf is tired, and will not answer any questions tonight. Now, if you will be so good as to allow us passage."

Your companion elbows her way through the assembled gathering and leads you to a seat. As soon as anyone tries to approach you she is on her feet, shooing them away with her umbrella. It is an amusing sight.

The harpist arrives. I busy myself with arranging chairs. It is only as she begins to play that I notice Leonard appear in the doorway. He looks round the room for you, sees you installed with your companion, then makes his way to the vacant place next to me. When there is a lull in the playing I lean toward him.

"Who is that woman with Virginia?"

He turns to me with a pained look on his face.

"Ethel Smyth."

I whisper back.

"The suffragette? Wasn't she in prison with Emmeline Pank-hurst?"

Leonard nods.

"And now she's an equally belligerent composer."

An arm reaches out and touches me and I look up abruptly. You stand in front of me, smiling.

"Nessa! This is the joy of having you back in England. Now we bump into each other in the street. I didn't even know you were in London."

My fingers dig into my pocket for Duncan's letter. The paper is razor sharp against my skin. My feelings are in such tumult that I scarcely trust myself to reply. You slip your arm through mine.

"Let's go and have tea."

Duncan's words spill and tumble round my mind. I need to be somewhere quiet to calm myself. I shake my head.

"I'm sorry," I blurt out, "I have to go to the . . . gallery."

You stare at me. I see that you are not taken in by my ruse.

"Well, lunch tomorrow, then. I'll expect you at one."

I stand rooted to the pavement. This is precisely the time Duncan has suggested I meet Peter. I try to recall the words he used to describe Peter's eyes. Something about grass once the snow has melted. I picture green against a retreating white, the blades yellowing from the loss of light.

"I can't, I'm going . . . What I mean is, I'm having lunch with Duncan." I cannot conceal my squalling emotions. You put your arm round my waist.

"Darling, what is it? There's something wrong. Don't hide it from me."

I let you lead me to a quiet bench in the middle of the square.

"I'm having lunch with Duncan. He's asked me to meet . . . Peter."

Your eyes light with understanding.

"He has no right!"

"No. I'm the one who requested it. He's doing it for me."

"But why?"

I look at the trees, the clouds fleeing across the sky. All the points of anchorage I have clung to seem to fissure and break above my head.

"Because . . . I can't bear not to see him."

For a moment neither of us speaks. Then your hand reaches for mine.

"At least let me come with you. That way there will be four of us. I can engage . . . this person . . . while you talk to Duncan."

I give your hand a squeeze.

"No. Thank you. It's kind of you to offer — but I have to face this alone."

I force myself to my feet. As I walk away I hear you call after me.

"I'll be in Rodmell this weekend. I'll come and see you. Sunday."

I cannot stop the pictures from forming in my mind. I push my stick into the river and watch the water eddy round it in fast-moving circles. If I close my eyes all I see is Duncan's face, smiling as he leans close to Peter. I step into the water and feel the icy cold seep into my shoes. The river is shallow near the bank and brown with mud. I walk forward, noting the rise in the level of the water. I stay close to the bridge, using its mass to screen me from view. It would be disastrous if anyone were to witness what I am about to do. I feel calmer now that I am in the water, as if the cold is slowly numbing my pain. This is what I desire. Not to feel anymore. Not to long for what I cannot have. I keep going until I am in the center of the river. The water is deeper here and I let the current catch hold of me. I surrender willingly as the river pulls me from my feet.

The persistent ringing of the doorbell brings me to my senses. I put my hands over my ears to block out the sound. I stare at the trail of muddy footprints my shoes have left on the floor, and wait for the intruder to leave. My clothes are torn and my legs and arms are covered in scratches. I raise my hand to my forehead and when I take it away my fingers are sticky with blood. Slowly, I recall the anesthetizing chill of the water. I remember the force of the current hurtling me toward the bridge, its vast underbelly looming ahead of me, the heave of the river tossing me into its grid. I do not know how long I remained wedged there, desperate to plunge back in. All I could think of was Duncan's declaration during the lunch with Peter that he could never make love to me again. I stared at the racing water and longed to be released into its embrace. Yet something — fear was it? — held me back. At some point I must have crawled, panting and exhausted, along the broad beam of a girder and hauled myself up onto the bank.

The ringing stops. There is a moment's silence, then I see your face at the window. Suddenly I remember. It is Sunday morning, the day you said you would come. You peer into the room. At last you find me and wave. I shrink into the shadows but it is useless. You go round to the French windows and let yourself through. When you realize the state I am in you hurry to my side.

"Nessa, darling. Whatever's happened to you? You're soaking wet. And covered in blood. Have you had an accident?"

I cannot answer.

"Did you fall in the river?"

Still I say nothing. Gradually the truth dawns on you.

"Oh, my God! What have you done?"

You help me undress and wrap me in a warm blanket. You stoke up the fire. Then you fetch water and a cloth from the kitchen and bathe the cuts on my head. You talk as you work.

"Why didn't you come to me? I can't bear to think what might have happened."

Now that you have something practical to do you seem not to mind that I do not reply. When you have finished dressing my wounds you fetch a bottle of brandy from the sideboard, and pour some into a glass.

"Drink this. It will help."

You lift the glass to my lips. I take a sip.

"I never imagined that you — I thought I was the only one who contemplated ending it all."

You let me catch my breath for a moment then lift the glass to my lips again.

"I always picture you happy — in the center of things."

The brandy is beginning to take effect. Thoughts of Julian, Quentin, Angelica surface in my mind. I try to speak.

"Will you promise me . . . ?

My voice is hoarse and you bend nearer.

"Dearest, anything."

"No, this is important."

It is painful to talk but I make myself continue.

"I want you to promise me that you will never tell any-one about this. I couldn't bear for the children to know. Or Duncan."

I pause.

"Promise me. That you will tell no one. Not even Leonard."

You clasp my hand.

"I promise — if you agree to promise something in return."

Your words catch me off-guard. I look at you and see that your eyes are full of tears.

"I want you to swear that no matter what happens — no mat-ter how terrible life is — you will never try anything like this again."

I nod. There is nothing in your tone to signal the import of the pact we are making.

Angelica kneels on the bed at my side. She has a tray in front of her, on which she has assembled an assortment of lipsticks, crayons, pots of powder, brushes. I feel the soft stroke of her fin-gers as she begins to work the colors over my face. She giggles as she applies patches of red, bars of pink, great blue stripes. She is re-creating me anew.

The room glitters with light. Most of the guests have already arrived and, like us, are costumed in an array of fantastical dis-guises. Angelica is trembling with excitement. The toile of her fairy skirt flutters as she hops from foot to foot, and the silver wings she has fastened to her back quiver as if at any moment she might fly. Clive, who has accompanied us to the party, dis-appears into the crowd. I watch him spinning from group to group like a child's top. I hold on to Angelica and steer her toward the refreshment table. A woman dressed in breeches with a pirate's patch over one eye waves. Immediately I change direction. It is too late. The figure bears down on us.

"Darlings! You look perfectly delicious! I could eat you both!" Lydia plants red lips on each of my cheeks before turning to Angelica.

"What an angel!" She links a hand through both our arms. The stuffed parrot on her shoulder lurches.

"Now, I demand all the news! Is it true that you and Duncan have been commissioned to decorate the royal yacht?"

Before I can contradict her, Lydia spies someone on the far side of the room and, with a final exhortation to help ourselves to water ices, dives back into the party.

To my relief I see you and Leonard standing by the window. We make our way across to you. You exclaim over Angelica's costume then turn to me.

"You look as if you have been Lydia'd."

"How Maynard can think of marrying such a creature is beyond me!"

We both laugh. You slip your arm through mine.

"Come on, let's leave Leonard and Angelica to fight for ices and find ourselves somewhere to sit."

We make our way to a quiet corner and settle ourselves on two empty chairs. You lean toward me.

"How are you feeling?"

I nod.

"Better. It's lovely having Angelica. Billy . . ."

You stop me, as if you know what I am struggling to say.

"Dearest, don't."

Before I can protest, Leonard is hurrying toward us, his face pale.

"I've left Angelica with Duncan," he begins by way of explanation. "I've just spoken to Mary. Lytton died this morning."

Instinctively, you reach for my hand. This is the news we have all been dreading.

"And Carrington?"

"Ralph is with her. She's in a terrible state, apparently."

For a moment no one speaks. The news is too abrupt, too raw. We all remember Carrington's suicide attempt when it first became clear that Lytton was seriously ill. You stare at the floor.

"I shall write to her. Ask her to come and stay."

Leonard sits beside you and puts his arm round you.

"Ralph is terrified of leaving her alone."

Suddenly you burst out.

"She must not be allowed to end it! Lytton loved her. As long as she lives, something of him — perhaps the best part of him — continues."

You are shaking like a leaf. Leonard looks at me.

"Shall I call a cab?"

I nod. It seems pointless going on with the party.

The bowl glides over the grass and comes to rest within a hair's breadth of the jack. Leonard, in his official capacity as referee, measures the distance then pronounces you the winner. You turn toward your opponents and bow.

"Angelica," I call, "will you help me bring out the tea?"

I see you whisper something in Angelica's ear. She nods then runs after me. We go into the kitchen together and I hand her a tray.

"Can you carry the cups and saucers for me and put them on the table?"

Angelica hovers awkwardly near the range.

"What is it?" I ask as I pour boiling water into the pot.

"Aunt Ginny says she's going to ask the fairies for money to buy me clothes," Angelica begins.

I fill the pot and give the tea leaves a stir.

"But you have lovely clothes." I struggle to keep my voice neutral.

Angelica shifts from one foot to the other.

"She said I could spend it on whatever I wanted to. I know we often don't have enough — and Aunt Ginny's very rich."

I flinch.

"We'll think about it," I say, putting the teapot and a plate of scones onto a second tray. "Now let's take this out into the garden before it gets cold."

I am uncomfortable all through tea. When it is over I encourage Angelica and Quentin to take Leonard for a walk. As soon as they are out of earshot I seize my chance.

"Angelica says you have offered to give her an allowance."

"Yes. She loves pretty things and I thought . . ."

"You thought you could barge in and do exactly as you pleased!"

"You're being unfair, Ness."

"Am I? If your intention really was to be kind you should have consulted me first. Don't think I don't see how you use her as a pawn."

You stop stacking the dirty cups and look up.

"I don't know what you're talking about."

"All those messages from the fairies meant for me. What are you trying to tell me now? That I am inadequate as a mother."

You look away. I begin to regret my outburst.

"Things are difficult enough between us at the moment."

I bite my lip, wondering whether to go on. You sense my hesitation.

"Angelica adores you. All your children do."

I shake my head.

"No, I don't mean that. Angelica's been asking questions about Clive."

You put the stacked crockery onto a tray.

"What sort of questions?"

"Oh, nothing very specific. She wants to know why Clive is always in London." I busy myself with the plates.

"She still doesn't know?"

I shake my head.

"Don't you think it's time you told her the truth?"

I stare at you, horrified.

"I couldn't possibly tell her! She's far too young. And in any case, think how difficult it would be for Clive. She has his name."

"She's going to find out sooner or later. She even looks like Duncan."

"Yes, but not yet."

"I don't understand how delaying will make it easier."

I look at you helplessly. Suddenly I blurt out the truth.

"I'm frightened Duncan wouldn't come at all if he felt there were ties on him as a father."

I pick up one of the trays and carry it across the garden. After a moment you pick up the second tray and follow me into the kitchen.

I have split myself between too many stools. No, that is not the right phrase — you always laughed at my inability to remember idioms correctly. Still, it is the thought that is uppermost in my mind as I wave goodbye to Angelica. I watch the car wind its way down the lane, straining for a final glimpse before it disappears from view. I remain for a moment in the doorway and look out across the garden. There is a mist over the pond and the light has the pearly quality of early morning. I turn back inside the house.

Now that Angelica is gone, I have the whole day for painting. I make my way down the hall and wander into the sitting room. I am not ready to go to my studio yet. I find a chair and remember the ambitions I had for my art before my children were born. The days and weeks of Angelica's school term stretch out ahead of me, but instead of relishing my longed-for freedom, I have no desire to work. The newspaper stares at me from the table. I resist the temptation to pick it up. I know it will be a distraction. I have to sit with my emptiness, find a way of reconnecting with the young woman I used to be.

I am working on two large canvases simultaneously. One of them is nearly finished, the other I have only just started. I move back and forth between them. The challenges I encounter in the new painting come as a welcome relief from the problems I am confronting in the earlier one. In the first picture, an elegantly dressed woman perches on a footstool in front of a fire. She is gazing at the naked figure of a small boy — her son, we suppose. There is a coolness in her look, an aloofness, as if she is holding something in check. On the right of the picture a second woman is seated on a sofa with a much smaller child. She is dressed in more workaday clothes than the first. Her flat, scuffed shoes contrast sharply with the other's polished leather and heels. Unlike the first woman, she is fully engaged with the child she is holding. She has her arms round him, trying to restrain him from reaching for a toy. The older boy stares at the child. Although his stance indicates that his attention is directed toward his mother, his head is turned away toward this child. The toys — a horse, a book, a boat — are arranged to fill the space between the figures, as if to eliminate any distance between them. The woman on the footstool has a mirror and handkerchief in her hand. I cannot decide if these are intended for the boy or are part of her own preparation for leaving. Something about the way she gazes at the boy tells us she will soon depart. There is resignation as well as wistfulness in her expression. She is studying the boy far too intently, instead of clasping him to her. It is as if she knows that in order to detach herself she must restrain from loving him.

There are no children in the second picture. Here my focus is exclusively the two women. On the left, a nude reclines on a sofa, resting, perhaps, from her work of posing as a model. On the right the woman is fully dressed, staring at the arrangement of fruit on the table before her. She might be the artist, though there is no sign of any painting materials and her clothes seem altogether too sophisticated. She appears utterly indifferent to the woman on the sofa. Whatever she finds in the fruit bowl preoccupies her entirely.

I cannot finish this second picture. There remains something vacant at its heart. I paint a stove and a coal scuttle, a second, lower table, a lamp and a vase of flowers, yet the void persists. I begin to sense that neither of the women is central to the painting: whatever work of art they are creating seems somehow beyond their reach. The woman on the sofa leans her head back against her arm. She looks tired, as if she would like to relinquish her role of artist's model and rest. The other woman stares at the fruit bowl as if its secret eludes her.

Perhaps it is her husband, or son, who is the painter, and she is merely an accessory, required to serve tea to his guests. The expression in her eyes suggests that she is unhappy with her lot. Her rapt concentration intimates that she, too, might have been an artist, if only the setting had been different, if only the places had been reversed. In the end, I abandon the picture. I cannot bear to go on with it. Something in the women's demeanor implies that I am responsible for their failure, that it is my task to alter their fate. Yet I scarcely know how.

There is a fireplace in the center, a window at one end, a small stove and washstand in a corner. I stack my parcels by the door and walk round the space. The bareness pleases me. Now that Angelica is away at school and I am on my own, I have decided to close up Charleston for part of each week and rent a studio in London near Duncan. I unwrap the first of my packages. It is one of Duncan's paintings, a jug of the orange and lemon branches he brought back as a gift from North Africa. I stand it on the shelf above the fireplace. Already, the mood of the room changes. I walk round it again, planning. I will have a bed here, doubling as a divan during the day, and set my easel opposite the window. I will buy an old screen and decorate it to close off the stove and washstand from the rest of the space. I imagine dark red curtains, patterned with gold leaves, walls the color of cream. There is no chair so I lodge on the windowsill and pull out my pencil and sketchbook. Within seconds I am drawing, my pencil flying over the paper as I struggle to keep pace with my vision. I feel a familiar sense of immersion.

One morning a cat appears in my studio through the open window. I offer him a saucer of milk which he eyes suspiciously.

I decide the best thing I can do is ignore him. I begin painting, aware, whenever I look up, of his green eyes studying me. After an hour or so the cat walks to the window, leaps to the sill, and disappears onto the roof. His desertion troubles me. As I rinse away the undrunk milk I feel I have failed a test.

The next day the cat returns. This time he accepts the saucer of milk and laps it up hungrily. Then he settles himself on his haunches to watch me work. I name him Marco Polo.

His visit becomes our daily routine. I find myself waiting for his arrival each morning. I grow accustomed to his piercing stare as I paint. We become friends of sorts. I find an old box and a blanket and clear a space for him near the stove. As I work I talk to him, describing my design or the problems I encounter in its execution. I have the strangest sense that he understands. Soon, his presence is indispensable to me. I find I cannot paint without his jewel-green eyes observing me. I admire his aloofness. I feel flattered that he has chosen me as a companion. Above all, his gaze returns me to those far-off days when we worked alongside each other in the conservatory at home, and plotted our future.

I am in your hall, looking for my cardigan, when the phone rings. I pick it up and listen to a voice describe the fall, the transfer to hospital, the unexpected heart attack. When the voice has said all it has to say I replace the receiver and stare at the number printed on a card on the dial. It is a number I half know and I try to think whose it could be. Then I remember that it is your number and Roger is dead and you and Leonard are waiting out on the terrace and do not know.

You see at once that something has happened. You raise your hand, as if to ward off the blow. The color drains out of your face as I tell you. We sit together in silence for a long time. Then Leonard gets up and goes quietly into the house. I turn to look at you. Your arms are hugged to your chest and you rock backward and forward in your chair like a child. I know, without needing to ask, that you are thinking, as I am, how brutal death is.

Images of Roger dance before me. I remember his energy, the bright music of his voice. I think how I spurned his love, took his friendship for granted. Suddenly I am screaming. I snap my eyes shut and dare not open them. I sense that if I do the light will destroy me. Though my eyelids are as frail as a moth's wings they are all that keep me from annihilation. I am terrified that at any moment they will blink open and I will be punished for my crime.

I become aware of your presence. You see that I am awake and come instantly to my side.

"Dearest, how are you feeling? Is there anything you would like?"

I shake my head.

"You've given us all a terrible fright."

I think of Duncan, the children, and try to speak. You pat my hand.

"Shh. Don't talk just yet. You need to drink something."

You take a glass from the tray by my bed and raise it to my lips. I gulp the water gratefully.

"There. That will help."

You put the glass back and sit beside me.

"How long have I been like this?" I whisper.

"Two days. You collapsed on the terrace and we decided the best thing would be to keep you here."

I clasp your arm.

"I can't bear the thought that I'll never be able to talk to him again."

"I know."

You search in your pocket and pull out a letter. I recognize Roger's handwriting.

"I've been reading his last letter. He wrote it after staying with you at Charleston." You take the sheets of paper out of their envelope. "He writes about you . . . the unique atmosphere you create round you — he says the beauty of your way of life sustains him."

I want to ask to see the letter but it is too soon. Instead, I gaze at the book lying open on your chair.

"Will you read to me?"

I hold on to your voice as you relate the story of Persephone's marriage to Hades. I imagine Demeter's desperate search for her daughter and the bargain struck with Zeus, then Persephone emerging from the Underworld, her eyes blinking against the vehemence of the light. I picture the pomegranate she carries in her hand, plucked from Hades' garden as she is set free. Was it a memento of her stay in the Underworld, I wonder, or a provision against Demeter having everything her own way?

I can lie to my daughter no longer. This is the thought that has been gathering force in my mind all day. I walk round the garden and watch a solitary blackbird peck for worms on the grass.

I take Angelica into the sitting room. Somehow it seems easier to tell her here. Together we admire a burst of purple crocuses under the trees. She says nothing as I speak. The only sign that she is listening is a sudden tightening of her hand on my arm. I want her to protest, ask me questions, blame me for concealing the truth. She does none of these things. When I have finished she slips her hand free and goes into the garden. As she makes her way across the lawn I see the blackbird again. It has a worm held prisoner in its beak. Later that evening I knock on Angelica's door. There is no answer, though I know she is there. I sit on the landing, hoping she will come out and talk. I wait in vain.

The world turns Chinese. On the radio, by chance, I hear a program on Hankow, the bustle of the streets and singsong of the market traders transmitted straight into my sitting room. I go to the exhibition on Chinese art at the Royal Academy and return with gaudily painted plates and a silk fan. I buy a map of China and learn its geography in idle moments.

Julian's letter announcing his intention to teach English in China arrives while I am in Cassis. I sense from his tone that this is a decision I cannot alter. I try to imagine three years without Julian and my mind balks at the thought. I hurry back to England to spend what time I can with him.

We stand together on the quay at Newhaven, waiting for the ferry. I dare not let go of Julian's arm. I know that once I do it will be a long time before I can touch him again. We make an odd couple. I am aware of the glances we are attracting. The whistle sounds and I hug Julian to me in a last embrace. He turns to wave as he boards the boat before disappearing into the crowd of passengers.

I drive to Charleston as slowly as I can. I dread the empty house. Once inside I go instinctively to Julian's room. I sit on his bed and look at his books and papers, a jacket left hanging on a peg. He will have a new landscape round him now, one I cannot as yet imagine. I take off my shoes and lie full length on the bed, reaching to pull the jacket from its peg. The coarse wool reminds me of the shawl Mother used to slip round her shoulders as she disappeared on a nursing errand. I remember the sight of the front door closing behind her and the hollow feeling in the pit of my stomach as I heard her feet run down the stone steps. I put the jacket on. I do not know how to bear this latest separation. I hear Father's voice calling Mother's name: "Julia! Julia!" Its echo with "Julian" strikes me for the first time.

The unfamiliar stamp on the envelope and my name and address in Julian's flowing hand give me an immediate jolt of pleasure. The thin paper crackles as I scoop the letter from the mat and carry it to the kitchen. My heart soars as I slit the envelope open and find several sheets inside. I take the pages out and lay them on the table. I am torn between wanting to savor this moment and my yearning to dive in and read.

Julian's letters become the high point of my week. I reread them until I feel as if I am beginning to know not only a different country, but also my son in a new way. It is as if the distance between us, the fact that we can only communicate by writing, encourages us to reveal more about ourselves than we have ever dared to before. I sense that Julian is telling me everything, holding nothing back. I revel in the full, luxurious unravelings of his heart and mind. I start to understand his feelings, anticipate his thoughts. It is a reciprocal process. I, in my turn, find myself pouring out all the old hurts in my letters, disclosing things it has always seemed impossible to tell. As the months pass, I become aware that our relationship is changing. Now it is Julian offering me advice, Julian pledging love and support. Life unfurls through my son.

There is not enough money to pay the excess postage. The postman waits patiently at the door, holding a parcel that I see straightaway is from Julian. I rummage in my purse, counting out the coins. Three shillings and eleven pence. I run down the hall into the kitchen and turn out the pot where Grace keeps the spare change from the shopping. Only another shilling and sixpence, still nowhere near enough. I go back to the door and press all I have into the postman's hand. He promises to return in the afternoon. I watch him take Julian's parcel away.

When the doorbell rings later that day I have the money ready. I thank the postman and take the package into my studio. Carefully, I cut open the string and brown paper. I gasp when I see what is inside. Neatly stacked one on top of the other are layers of brilliantly colored Chinese silks. I let my fingers run across them, relishing their smoothness. Splashes of red, green, blue, yellow, orange, pink, mauve spill from the paper. I imagine Julian choosing the colors, watching as the lengths are cut from the rolls and folded into squares. I pick up one of the silks and shake it free. It is a blue so deep it is almost black where its folds lie in shadow. I drape it over the back of my chair. I shake out a second length of cloth. This one is orange and its burst is so intense I can feel it burning my eyes. I unravel length after length until the room shimmers with color. It is as if I have let a rainbow out of the parcel. I tie one of the silks round my waist, loop another over my arms. I knot one in my hair and thread yet another round my shoulders. I look at myself in the mirror and laugh out loud at the picture I make. I want to dance for pure joy. I spend the entire afternoon absorbed with my package, trying the silks in fresh combinations. I delight in the way the colors harmonize and clash with each other, setting off different resonances, creating new blends. When it is time to go downstairs I fold each length of silk back into a square. Then I pull open a drawer and tip out all the sketches I have stowed there. I lay the silks in the drawer, placing a fresh sheet of paper between each one. When the last is safely packed away I close the drawer. I do not open it again in Julian's lifetime.

10

I STAND BY YOUR WINDOW AND LOOK OUT OVER THE
trees of the square. You have been called down to the base-
ment for some problem connected with the press. I do not
know how long you will be gone. I turn away from the window and walk slowly round the room. On the far wall are the
three large panels Duncan and I painted together shortly after
you moved in here. I stare at them now, trying to assess them
with a critical eye. The colors are Mediterranean — red, blue,
brown — the still lifes enclosed in a roundel bordered by cross-
hatching. I study the objects: the table, jug, and scroll of paper
on my left; the piano and guitar ahead of me; the vase of flowers, open book, fan, and mandolin to my right. I attempt to re-
kindle my mood of tranquil absorption as I worked alongside
Duncan.

You come back into the room, frowning.

"Is everything all right?" I ask.

"Yes. Some muddle over an order. Fortunately, when I
looked, Leonard's directions were perfectly clear." You sit in

your customary chair. The dogs, who have been curled on the rug in front of the fire, get up and lie beside you. You let your hand rest on Pinker's head.

"We've had letters from Julian. One for Leonard and one for me. They came yesterday."

I start. This is precisely the topic I have been hoping to talk to you about.

"What does Julian say? Is he well?"

"He sounds as if he's bent on proving himself. Leonard's letter particularly is all about politics. He wants to use the Labour Party as a platform for an armed revolution — and he wants Leonard to help him do it!"

Your words make me blanch. For weeks now, all Julian's letters have described is his increasing frustration at the wait-and-see attitude of the Left.

"He says Europe has only two choices — we can either surrender to the fascists or else we must fight. He thinks decisive military action is the only hope for Spain." I bite my lip. "Is this what you and Leonard think? It seems to contradict everything we struggled for during the last war." To my surprise, you turn away. I watch you fondle Pinker's ears.

"Oh, we argue about it too," you say vaguely. You raise your hand to sweep a stray strand of hair back into place. Pinker, who has been enjoying your caresses, lifts her head.

"I'm worried about Julian," I blurt out. You swivel round in your chair.

"Why?"

"Everything he says is so black and white. I'm worried that the distance — the fact that he's isolated and so far away — means the reality of the situation is lost on him."

"It certainly seems to give him a false sense of what he can achieve!" You do nothing to hide your exasperation. "Even his idea of going to Spain is only a stepping stone — a way of gaining firsthand military experience, which he can then use in a more grandiose scheme!"

"But he still has another year to run on his contract . . ." So far in his letters Julian's comments about Spain have been hypothetical. You realize my alarm.

"Do you remember the war games he and Quentin used to play when they were little? That's what his letters remind me of now. The frustrations of a small boy dressed up as military strategy. Did I ever tell you about the last time he came here? I was on my own and as I looked down the stairs into the hall I saw a strange man. I called down and asked who it was, and it was only when he looked up that I saw it wasn't a strange man at all — just Julian wearing an enormous hat. He never did care how he dressed. He wanted a phone number — I can't remember whose — and I invited him to come up and have lunch with me. He shook his head and muttered something about having too much to do, though I could tell he was pleased to be asked. Afterward it occurred to me that this was the crux of the problem: how does a young man surrounded by a family who adores him ever succeed in breaking free?"

"Did he tell you he's having an affair?" I ask suddenly. You grin.

"Well then that's good, isn't it? I know how much you and he mean to each other but at some point he has to live his own life."

I stare at my hands. The nails are rough and split though I have done no work today.

"When he first went to China I missed him terribly. Then his letters started arriving. They seemed to give him back to me."

"There's nothing wrong in writing . . ." you begin. For once I do not wish to be exonerated, and I press on with my point.

"I do see that I've hung on to him too hard. I wanted the best for all my children, but perhaps especially for Julian. He was my firstborn. Sometimes I think that everything I do ends up damaging them. It's as if I can't see them as separate people — only as part of myself. The best part." I let my hands drop to my lap. You gaze at me in silence for a moment.

"The fact that he's involved with another woman suggests you haven't damaged Julian all that much."

I shake my head.

"It isn't a real relationship. None of his affairs are. She's the wife of his professor."

"Does he know?"

"Of course not. But it can only be a matter of time before he finds out."

"And the consequences?"

"He'll be forced to leave. I'm certain of it."

I walk back to the window. I decide to try one last appeal.

"Billy, will you write to Julian for me? Persuade him that no matter what happens he mustn't go to Spain. I don't think I could bear it if anything happened to him."

I look straight into your eyes. To my relief, you nod.

I keep myself busy. Duncan persuades me to see the surrealist exhibition with him in London and I go, despite my dislike of their work. I realize as soon as I enter the room that coming was a mistake. I choose a canvas almost at random and spend several minutes examining it; I know that one cannot look at a painting quickly. There is a hand in close-up on the left, the huge thumbnail turned toward us. The fingers hold a bizarre contraption concocted from what appears to be a walnut shell and metal pins. Some of the pins pierce the finger through. There are two heads on the right of the picture. The eyes are bloodshot and appear to be human, though the shape of the heads suggests birds. One of the heads has a pair of horns to which a string is attached. At the top there is a balloon, a black dot in the sky.

I do not like this picture. All my painter's instincts reject the obtrusive symbolism, the fragments of a narrative that thwart my desire to see. Despite my objections, my mind races with possible interpretations. Is this the hand of God in close-up on the left? Are the birds a pair? What am I to make of the cruel contraption? Or the balloon, floating apparently freely in the distance? This is not painting, I want to shout; this is pictorial inquisition. It forces us to think, not to look. It is the antithesis of all I have ever prized in art. I make my way to the exit.

The cool of the street refreshes me. I know that Duncan will remain in the exhibition for some time and I go to the park while I wait. I walk for several minutes before stopping to rest on a bench by the pond. The roses are in full bloom; their heavy perfume scents the air. I take out my sketchbook and pencil case and draw the fountain. There are birds perching on the statue at its center. As I work I realize to my horror that I have reproduced the birds' heads from the painting. The string I have unwittingly tied to the horns of the smaller bird looks like a bridle, as if it is there to prevent flight. I sketch in the God-like hand. Are these the fingers of a man or woman, I wonder? I draw the walnut shell, faithfully inserting the largest of the pins through the thumb. Only in my picture there is blood. I find a crayon and work a gash of red, contorting the thumb as it registers the stab of pain. I tear the sheet from my book and start again, this time the careful copy of a rose. I work the scallop shell of the outer petals, the tight whorl at its heart. I am quiet now, reproducing my rose. I continue with my drawing until it is time to return to the exhibition to find Duncan.

Julian's words become reality. My thoughts jar and wrestle each other as I read his letter announcing his intention to fight for the Communists in Spain. He asks me to travel to Cassis so that we can meet when his ship docks at Marseilles. I respond at once, sensing there is little time. I point out that there are others who have a claim on him in England apart from me. I remind him of Charleston, the sunny corner in the sitting room where he likes to read, his favorite walks across the downs. I fold the letter into its envelope and put it in my pocket. On my way to the post I pull the petals from a wild dog rose flowering in the hedgerow and press them between the sheets of my letter. My petition works; Julian agrees to come home. For the time being, at least, he is safe.

I organize a party for his homecoming. Julian, wearing Chinese robes, presides in the place of honor. I cannot stop looking at him. It is as if I need to feast my eyes after all the months of separation. He dispenses the presents he has brought for us. I have silks and hand-pressed paper; Duncan and Quentin have drawings, Angelica a doll's size porcelain tea set. There are books for you and Leonard and Clive. We ask about China until there are no more questions. Julian describes landscapes, people, unfamiliar customs, the idiosyncrasies of the language, as if he has rehearsed every word. We talk until late at night. Quentin tries on Julian's robes, and Angelica is taught the correct posture for a Chinese lady. Even you appear intrigued by Julian's account of his writing friend Su-Hua. After everyone has gone to bed, I remain at the empty table and issue a silent prayer that such happiness will last.

The next day Julian and I walk over the downs. We link arms, like old lovers. He breaks the news I have been dreading. He says he cannot bear to sit idly by while the government does nothing, and all the while the fascists increase their hold. He mentions the names of others who have gone. He tells me he has weighed the risks and is ready to lay down his life for a cause he fully supports.

We fight like wild beasts. I did not know it was possible to fight so long or so hard. We fight until late at night when we retreat to bed exhausted, our arguments in stalemate, only to return at first light with restored energy and fresh ammunition for a new attack. I deploy every weapon I can think of. When my own powers of persuasion fail, I call on you, Clive, Maynard, to step in. At length we beat out a weary compromise. Julian will not enlist with the International Brigade but will join Spanish Medical Aid as a volunteer driver.

It is the best I can do. I have used every tactic at my disposal. All I can hope for, now, is to limit the risk. I watch Julian disappear in the ambulance he has raised money to buy and equip, and clutch hold of the gatepost. I am not sure how long I stay like this. All I know is that when I go back into the house it is dark. I turn on the lamps and stoke the fire in the sitting room, searching for something to do. Finally I go out into the garden, hoping that here, in the stillness, I will recapture a little of the serenity I felt when Julian first came home.

I focus in on the house. It soothes me to be amongst Julian's things and I decide to redecorate his room. I am struck by how tidy he has left everything. His desk is bare, his clothes folded and stowed away in the chest. I take his books down from the shelves and stack them in boxes. I move the bed away from the window and cover it with an old sheet. Then I prepare my paints. I do not think as I work, but force myself to concentrate on the colors and shapes before me. I design a frieze round the window, gray vases filled with lilies, the symbols of peace. Above the pelmet I paint yellow suns circled by blue dots. I fill the spaces between the suns with brown latticework, smaller circles, red and white flowers. Suddenly, from out of the corner of my eye, I see something move. For a moment I think it must be Quentin, but as the face tilts toward me I realize it is Julian. I spin round, incredulous. The figure vanishes. I stand stock still, one hand on the window ledge to steady myself. I look carefully round the room. There is nothing there. My eye comes to rest on a small key that has been left in the lock in the top drawer of Julian's desk. I take the key out, intending to put it somewhere for safekeeping. My movement pulls the drawer, which is not locked, partly open. There is a pile of papers inside. On top is a note with the words "to be opened in the event of my death" in Julian's hand.

Once again, I contrive to keep busy. Quentin writes a play for my birthday. We take our places in the sitting room, where the chairs have been arranged in a semicircle. Angelica stands in front of the fireplace, wearing a conical hat marked with the word "guide." She is carrying a number of sheets of paper and proceeds to label us, as if we are items of furniture. Clive, Bunny, and Maynard are tagged, then you, Leonard, Duncan, and me. Without my glasses I find it hard to make out what the labels say. Quentin appears and reads a story from a newspaper concerning a delegation of visitors from the moon. It seems we are in the year 2036. Angelica welcomes Quentin to Charleston and takes him on a tour of the room. She points out that the decorations were achieved using an ancient technique of pot and brush. Quentin yawns, visibly bored by her explanations. It is only when Angelica begins to talk about the occupants of the house that Quentin registers an interest. His appetite whetted, he probes his guide for information about their personalities and habits. His eyes grow round as she tells him about my proclivity for receiving guests in clothes spattered with paint or mud from the garden. No one is spared. Your dislike of being photographed is held up for ridicule, as are Leonard's summary refusals to join in a game. Spurred on by her interrogator, Angelica reveals more and more of our foibles. She exposes Clive's leisurely morning toilette, Duncan's inability to commit to an engagement, Maynard's miserliness with money. As the play draws to a close we clap and cheer and demand an encore. No one has mentioned the fighting in Spain for almost an hour.

We stroll into the garden, where a table has been laid with food. I find you sitting on a rug under one of the apple trees. I plant myself next to you.

"Angelica has talent," you begin. "She could go far."

"She adores acting. She always has."

"She's very good at it." You turn so that you are looking at me directly. "I wasn't the only one to notice how entrancing she was in that white shift."

"What do you mean?"

"Bunny couldn't take his eyes off her!"

"Bunny? Don't be ridiculous."

"For a painter I sometimes wonder at the things you don't see."

"Bunny has known Angelica ever since she was born. He could be her father. Besides, he was only invited because we were all so moved by his letter." I pull a daisy from the grass. "It seems Barbara hasn't much longer to live."

"Precisely." You stare at me coolly. "Did you miss the way he smiled at her when she pinned on his label?"

I cannot hide my indignation.

"Of course I noticed! She couldn't get the pin through the wool of his jacket so he helped her tuck the paper under his lapel."

Your face breaks into a wry smile.

"I sometimes feel as if we see the world through the same pair of eyes — only we're wearing different glasses."

"Talking about glasses, I couldn't read the labels. Were you meant to be a bookcase?"

You give me a roguish wink.

"Ha! I was Fiction!"

The prospect of another war looms closer. Julian's letters start to arrive. In contrast to his expansive, measured, often self-reflective writings from China, these are terse, decisive, and give the impression of being dispatched at tremendous speed. I arrange them on the mantelpiece like a charm. I have the superstitious notion that the longer the line grows, the safer Julian will be.

I invite Wogan to visit. Though his arm is still heavily bandaged, I press him to tell me about the fighting. He describes the waiting, the bursts of frenzied activity, the almost casual attitude to death.

I stop writing and stare out the sitting room window. The swallows are wheeling in erratic patterns overhead. I take off my glasses and rub my aching forehead. What I am about to relate requires all my courage.

This is my picture of Julian's final day. Waking early, the sun already hot, and taking advantage of a lull in the fighting to fill in some of the potholes that obstruct the route to the front. Diving for cover as a group of enemy planes appear, their gunfire whipping the road into dust. A shell exploding near the ambulance where Julian has taken refuge. The shock as a fragment of casing sears into his flesh. The attempt to write to me, three hastily scribbled words on an empty page of his notebook.

When the telephone call comes I cannot take in what the voice is telling me. The blood pounds in my ears, my breath heaves in painful gasps. After that, everything is black. It is as if the water has closed round me at last.

Once again, you save me. You, sitting by my bed, stringing your words. I cling to them as to a lifeline. I cannot think, I cannot speak, I can only listen. At first, I do not understand what your phrases mean. Then, one evening, I think I see Julian's dead body laid out on an operating table and I turn to you screaming. You hold me tight in your arms. The world is a work of art, I hear you say, and though there is no God we are parts of the design.

I glimpse the hand with its contraption. I sense that as one of us surrenders, the other must fight. I witness the blood the struggle causes. And in the distance, like a chimera, I spy a brilliantly colored, free-floating balloon.

11

I SEAT MYSELF AT JULIAN'S DESK. I HAVE POSTPONED this moment for long enough. I slide the key into the lock, open the top drawer, and take out his papers.

You are right, Julian's memoir should be published. I have a folder of his poems, another of his letters. I owe it to my son to salvage something lasting from his life. I pick up the first sheet on the pile. The sight of Julian's handwriting is still too painful. I put the papers back in the drawer and write to ask if you will edit them for me.

You come to tea. I am making blackout curtains, the heavy material draped over my knee. I do not look up as you settle yourself beside me.

"How are you feeling?" you ask after a moment.

I push my needle into the fabric and pull the thread through.

"Can I help?"

I shrug. You take my gesture as a sign of acquiescence. From the corner of my eye, I watch you begin to hem the curtain from the opposite end to where I am working. We sew in silence for some minutes.

"Did I tell you I've had a letter from Helen about the cottage?" you begin. I almost jab the needle into my finger. I am so angry I burst out.

"Helen wrote to me herself. She said you had practically begged her to take it! You have no right!" You look up quickly. My vehemence has surprised you.

"Helen was looking for a cottage — so I thought I'd suggest it. She and her children seem an amiable sort."

"Only because you won't be living in fear of their knocking on your front door every two minutes! Or of bumping into them whenever you go out!

"I didn't realize you had taken so violently against Helen."

"It isn't Helen. You had no business mentioning it to anyone." I finish my thread and sew the end fast.

"I'm sorry. I thought if someone you knew took the cottage you wouldn't feel so isolated. Duncan says you've had no visitors for weeks."

I refill my needle and pull another pleat of fabric onto my knee. You steady your end of the curtain with your hand.

"You used to love having people round you. This house was always full of guests. You're in danger of becoming a recluse."

I adjust my seam so it is straight.

"I've had enough of people."

"I don't understand why you're shutting yourself away. You used to be —"

"I know, the source of light," I interrupt rudely.

"Duncan tells me you're not painting either."

I stare at my needle, pushed halfway through the cloth. What you say is perfectly true. I have painted very little since Julian died.

"So?"

"Ness, you've always painted."

"Well perhaps it's time I gave up."

"Don't say that." Your voice has dropped to a whisper.

"It's true. Everything I paint is ugly, dead. No point carrying on."

You have gone pale. I feel a stab of guilt. I know you cannot bear to see me like this.

"No one is buying paintings anyway."

"No one is buying books, but that hardly seems a reason not to write!"

I glance up. For the first time it occurs to me that the war will make a difference to you.

"Do you believe there's any truth in the rumors about invasion?"

"I think it's perfectly likely." You have stopped sewing too. We stare at each other for a moment. "The other night as I lay awake I imagined it happening. I heard tires on the gravel, a knock on the door, shouts in German as soldiers entered the hall."

"And Leonard?"

"He says this time we're the frontline." You take the scissors and trim some frayed ends from the edge of the cloth.

"You've heard the reports. Jews rounded up and interned. Leonard wouldn't have a chance."

"And you?"

To my surprise, you laugh.

"The mad wife of a Jew! I don't fancy my chances either."

"But what can we do?" Our seams are almost touching. You fold in your side of the curtain.

"Be ready. Leonard has a hose and an extra can of petrol in the garage."

Now it is my turn to blanch. Your calmness astounds me. You scarcely seem afraid.

It is as if a giant has reached down and torn the wall off a doll's house. The central spine of the staircase still stands, but behind it all I can see are the remains of rooms, a mirror with its glass smashed hanging over a fireplace, the legs of a table poking through a mound of rubble, an overturned bath. Though there have been pictures of the London bombings in the papers, nothing has prepared me for this. The building has been roped off and a warden comes toward me as I approach. I explain who I am and she lets me pass. As we climb the stairs I feel as if the entire edifice could collapse at any moment. I press my scarf to my nose to protect myself from the dust. When we reach my landing I see the door to my studio has been blown off its hinges. With the warden's help I wrench it free and step over a heap of fallen debris. Inside, it is as if the giant has ransacked everything I possess. My couch has been flung against the wall, my easel broken and upended, the crockery and books from my shelves strewn across the floor. I realize at once that my paintings are beyond repair. I stare at what is left of a canvas I must have propped under the window. The images have deformed into grotesque caricatures in the heat from the blast. I turn away. There is nothing to salvage here.

The book feels solid and heavy in my hands. I turn it over and stare at my son's name on the front cover. I carry it to the bookcase and let my finger run across the spines. This is not the only book you have made for me. At last I find what I am looking for. I pull out your biography of Roger and open it at the first page. I read your description of his childhood garden, the stunted and grimy apple tree, the poppies flowering by chance in a corner. Your words take me back to Cambridge, to a seat on a train and an as yet unknown man. The train races through the fields and the man calls out "Look, look!" I follow his gaze, and marvel at crimson poppies aflame against the ripening wheat. I am a young woman again, Julian is still a boy. Your words have this power.

You write on the anniversary of Julian's birthday. You are the only one to remember. I sit with your card on my knee and think about my children. Angelica is staying with Bunny, Quentin is in London; Duncan is working as a war artist in Plymouth and I do not expect him home. Though there has been no announcement as yet I know that Bunny will marry Angelica. Despite your words of comfort, I feel utterly bereft. I stare out of the sitting room window and watch the clouds scuttle across the sky. There seems little point in going on.

I put the key into the ignition and feel a flicker of hope as the engine pulses into action. I have to see you. I do not care that I am using my last ration of petrol. I have to tell you that I cannot be held to a promise I made when the circumstances of my life were very different.

I keep the car to a steady speed as I drive through the lanes. The trees cast dappling patterns onto the surface of the road. As I pull up in front of your house, the great elms, the ones you call Leonard and Virginia, wave to me in greeting. To my relief, you are alone.

I gaze round your sitting room in astonishment. There are boxes, piles of books, scattered papers everywhere. Then I remember that your London house has been bombed and realize that these must have come from the wreckage.

"Was the damage very bad?" I ask.

You kneel beside a box, and begin to remove the contents. You do not look at anything but simply add what you find to the avalanche already accumulating on your floor.

"Oh, everything smashed. Furniture, paintings, rugs — all destroyed. The books and papers were almost the only things that survived." You blow a thick layer of dust from a book. "As you see, even they aren't completely unscathed."

"Don't you think it would be better to leave them in the boxes?"

You look at me as if I am mad.

"Oh no, I have to get everything out."

"I'm sorry about the house."

"Don't be. In many ways it's a relief to be free of all those possessions. I've made discoveries too." You rummage in the pile beside you and pull out a notebook. "Look, here's the diary I kept while I was writing *To the Lighthouse*." You leaf through the pages, pausing to read some of the passages silently to yourself.

"Billy, there's something I want to say." I hesitate for a moment. "I . . . can't go on any longer."

You glance up. I watch your pupils dilate with fear. Instead of answering, you dive back into your box and bring out a packet of letters.

"Ah, these are the letters you wrote to me just before Thoby was born."

I cannot tell if your slip over Julian's name is deliberate. You take a letter from its envelope.

"Cleeve House! Do you remember old Squire Bell? That horse's hoof he had made into an ashtray. What a way to commemorate your favorite animal!"

"Billy." I am pleading with you now. "Do you remember that promise I made you?"

Still you ignore me. I know what you are doing, digging yourself into your story. I listen to your voice prattle on until it is time for me to leave. It is too dangerous to travel at night. Your body feels frail in my arms as I kiss you goodbye. For a moment I long to stay and stretch out beside you in front of the fire, feeding you thick slices of toast as I did when we were girls. Instead, I walk to my car and drive away.

It is your gardener who telephones. I hear his voice as if from a great distance. I replace the receiver and stare at the jug of flowers on the hall table. I do not know what to do with these words. They ricochet round my head yet they make no sense. Things are slipping away from me: the hall table and all the objects on it are careering out of reach. I lean back against the wall to steady myself. I see you standing on the riverbank, casting about for stones to fill your pockets. I feel the paralyzing cold as you wade in, the weight of your wet clothes as you force yourself forward. The water is in my mouth, my lungs, as the river drags us under. This time I cannot escape. The darkness has engulfed the picture. I have no will to defeat it.

12

I AM FOUR YEARS OLD, RUMMAGING THROUGH MOTHER'S work basket in the drawing room in St. Ives. Mother is sewing in her chair. For once, she and I are alone. I pull out one of her shawls and drape it over my shoulders. The shawl is soft and warm and smells of the lavender water Mother dabs on her wrists and temples whenever she is tired. I imagine I am a queen dressing for some important state occasion and tug at Mother's skirt to look. When she sees what I am wearing she tears the shawl away. In an angry voice she tells me her shawl is not for playing in and sends me out of the room. I stumble into the garden, trying not to cry. Thoby finds me and pulls me onto the grass, where we lie with our arms laced round each other's neck. I feel soothed and comforted, and as I gaze up at the clouds I spy angels. Then a shadow falls and you try to lie between us. I turn over and press my fists into my eyes. When I look again, you are on top of the garden wall with Thoby, waving.

This is the pattern I come back to. No matter how many times I shake the pieces, they always fall in the same places. Me, Thoby, you.

Charleston looks strangely desolate as the car drops me at the gate. I let myself in through the front door and glance at the letters Grace has left in a neat pile for me on the hall table. I make my way upstairs and stop outside the guest room. I go in and lie down on one of the beds. This is where Julian and Quentin slept when they were little. There is one of Angelica's paintings on the back of the door, a terra-cotta bust by Quentin on the windowsill. I pull the cover over me and close my eyes. I do not know how long I remain here. I think of the hopelessness of Leonard's expression as we buried your ashes under the elms. I become aware of people moving round me — Duncan, Quentin, Angelica, a stream of faces that intermingle and blur. Once, when I open my eyes, I see my own face in the dressing table mirror opposite the bed. My reflection in the silvered glass reminds me of another face, glimpsed what now seems a lifetime ago. I sit up slowly. It was in this mirror that I watched Mother die.

I begin with the vertical supports of my easel, solid parallel bars. Across them I work the horizontal struts, then finally the stand. Once I have the frame in place, I paint the reverse side of my canvas. I do nothing to disguise its blankness nor embellish its ugliness; what is important is that it covers the central space. To the right of the easel I paint myself, seated on my old chair, the one with the faded green cushion. Around me is the paraphernalia of painting: brushes and rags, my palette and mixing dishes, bottles of oil and turps. I tilt my head away from the easel, leaving the features of the face indistinct. I do not want the focus to be the artist but the act of painting itself. Above me, running right across the top of the picture, are the windows, with the pale sky and bare trees beyond. After I have been working for some time I pause to assess what I have done. There is the frame of the easel, the daunting emptiness of the canvas, the relative frailty of eye and brush and hand. I look again and discern a soft apricot, a flush of purple spilling through the lace curtain and onto the artist's sleeve. Her posture has an energy and resolution that remind me of you. I examine her figure more closely. This time, I realize that what she holds in her hand is not a brush, but a pen.

I work on a cover for your final novel. I draw curtains pulled across a stage, showing the fall of the fabric with quick marks of my pen. The sides dissolve into an abundance of flowers. I want to suggest that the play will be engrossing and rich. I put the title of your book at the top, making the words part of the design. I write our names, distinctly, proudly. I wonder if I should allow a gap in the curtains so that we glimpse something of the drama. What was it you said? It is not what we put in the frame that endures. I leave the curtains closed.

There is a vase of daffodils on my desk, a pool of molten gold against the wood. Soon I will paint them. Already, I am beginning to plan my colors. For now, I put my sketchbook aside. I have a few more sentences to add to my story.

13

~──────~

THERE, IT IS DONE. IN A MOMENT I WILL COLLECT MY pages together and tie them in a bundle. I will put on my jacket and boots and walk down to the river. Gathering up my skirt, I will kneel on the bank and look about me to ensure I am alone. I will dip the first sheet in the water, watching as my words begin to blur. I must wait until the paper is soaked so that it cannot blow away in the wind. Then I will let the current snatch it from my fingers. Only when all the pages have been released will I make my dedication. This story is for you.

My eye travels to the window and I am caught by a blaze of daffodils under the apple trees. I resolve to take my easel outside and paint these instead. I gaze at the yellow, vivid and tangible in the sunlight. You are right. What matters is that we do not stop creating.

ACKNOWLEDGMENTS

Although this is a work of fiction, it is indebted to the research of numerous critics and scholars, and in particular to four extraordinary biographies: Frances Spalding's *Vanessa Bell*, Angelica Garnett's *Deceived with Kindness: A Bloomsbury Childhood*, Jane Dunn's *Virginia Woolf and Vanessa Bell: A Very Close Conspiracy*, and Hermione Lee's *Virginia Woolf*. It also owes an immense debt of gratitude to the following institutions: the University of St. Andrews; the Leverhulme Trust; and Robinson College, Cambridge. Many individuals helped with this novel, including colleagues in the School of English at the University of St. Andrews, the team at New Writing Partnership (particularly Sally Cline and Michelle Spring), Ian Blyth, Alex Bulford, Jane Goldman, Jackie Kay, Eric Langley, Heidi Stalla, Helen Taylor, Jeremy Thurlow, and Molly Thurlow. Especial thanks are due to my agent, Jenny Brown; to my publishers, Sharon Blackie and David Knowles at Two Ravens and Lindsey Smith at Houghton Mifflin Harcourt; to Sara Lodge; and to my dear friend and mentor, Jo Campling. It is a source of deep regret that she did not live to see this project published. Finally, this novel owes everything to those two remarkable sisters, Vanessa Bell and Virginia Woolf, whose lives and works continue to intrigue, inspire, and delight.